To Weave a Grasshopper's Cage

Zdravka Evtimova

Fomite
Burlington, VT

ISBN-13: 978-1-959984-81-8
Library of Congress Control Number:
Fomite
58 Peru Street
Burlington, VT 05401

03-26-2025

THE SHADOWS OF OUR houses crept towards each other, very slowly, like schoolboys in love, silly and very beautiful — late snow in late March, the shadows of two houses, dark as a kiss, rushing off eagerly yet timidly down the backyard.

To creep into the hole in the hedge I had painstakingly made, I would cut twig after twig in the middle of the night, sometimes leaf after leaf as I turned into a shadow. I dragged myself on my belly, and the thin branches of the hedge bit me. Like radioactive rays killing a tumor — that was how the thorns dug into the skin of my back through my blouse. It hurt. The wounds were hard to heal. But I crawled and crawled closer to Nikolai. He was very handsome. God, what anemic words! He was so handsome that the moon melted in the sky when he appeared on the balcony of their house.

The sky would fall apart if I didn't see Nikolai go for a walk in his garden. He was so good-looking. I'd sneak up on him, me, from my part of town, the North District, the eight-story grey blocks of tiny flats where cockroaches crawled on your pillow. I crossed the 'gardens' between the buildings, paths beaten through the mud that had long forgotten what grass was, streets clogged up with discarded plastic bottles and cars, most over fifteen years old, bought dirt cheap from some pre-bankruptcy used car dealer in Germany, France or Austria, bone-shakers that left thick smoke in their wake. Everywhere in the "North parts", the clunkers were the first to rise up in the morning — with a powerful rumbling, their exhaust pipes spitting drops of foul-smelling liquid.

There was no time for the sun to shine. Exhaust fumes enveloped it like a glove, turning its luster into a dark grey orb. Summer in the North District was a dirty ball of reptiles, stray dogs, oldsters living on meager pensions, clutching at any straws available; guys counting their bucks to the next paycheck; women knowing money didn't grow on trees and saving every crumpled banknote a lover gave them after a beautiful night.

I used to walk all the way across the North District to the VIP area. That was the name of the southern, very narrow, negligibly small part of the city. VIP meant important people, people who expressed themselves exquisitely in English. Everybody in the city, even in the "North," believed they could speak the language as glibly as Shakespeare, bus drivers and lumberjacks though they were. In these parts, you could make a huge bundle if you jabbered English after a fashion. Often the bundle wasn't good at all, still, coins remained in your pocket. Even the old geezers over eighty most of them, would open their mouths after they caught a glimpse of a well-dressed woman, and instead of "Good morning," they shouted at her, "Hi, baby, how's it going?"

Of course, bodyguards kept a close watch, and wireless security cameras were scattered thickly throughout the VIP neighborhood.

Inside the VIP zone, were eleven mansions dubbed "the residences", or "the swan buildings". Black cars as huge as space shuttles, whose exhaust pipes emitted no stench, approached the gated compounds. The imposing gates swung open noiselessly as if they had been made of cat paws. The imposing vehicles confidently sank into the VIP property. To them, it was a hot bath.

How was it possible for me to slip in there, into Nikolai's room? He was a young male so magnificent that the car wipers refused to clean the windshield so everybody could admire him when he showed up in the coffee shop. The cleaning women in his house discussed his green eyes. The flawless skin of his face they said was as soft as the air on the days when the North wind blew, and the smoke curled upwards from Bare Mountain.

I snuck into the forbidden zone, for I was desperate. I had no friends, and my loneliness was as intense and troublesome as a narrow shoe. I was so used to it that if I bumped into anyone, or worse — if anyone took an interest in me, I'd beat a hasty retreat and wouldn't look back. I knew they'd deceive me, they'd find a way to lay their hands on the meager savings I'd been hiding under a pile of Mom's old sneakers before she'd married her Greek husband. I had a *bundle* as thin as a laser beam tucked away under my father's faded shirts. He had managed to marry an elderly Spanish woman too rich for her good. He expected her to die any day now, all to no avail, alas. The signora wasn't thinking of cashing in her chips.

On the other hand, how could I know if the Spanish milady was elderly or not? My father lied about everything under the sun. Maybe she was a young señorita, a belly dancer, and didn't have a penny to bless herself with. He'd probably latched onto her because he was a fool in love, an ugly insult to the phrase "in love". It was the shadows of the houses that fell in love as they crept quietly at dusk to kiss each other. The shadows had no money. They were made of air and cared nothing about interest rates or banks. Maybe that was the reason I'd been a shadow all my life — if cutting branches in the VIP's hedge was equal to living.

I'd been looking for another quiet, beautiful shadow to crawl to and kiss. Finally, I found what I'd been dreaming of — Nikolai. I saw him get out of a car, a black one, powerful as death, and I knew he was my shadow.

To land near the fence of prickly, perfectly trimmed bushes, I had to befriend Zoe, that perpetually complaining bag of cosmetics layered on an expressionless face. Zoe was a boss of no influence at one of the numerous ministries in our country — so dismissively petty was she that sucked up even to me. Only later did I realize how dumb I had been. She was subservient to me because of her son, Rosen. She hoped that her kid, an unbalanced individual, suffering from some subtle form of insanity, would marry me. I was slow on the uptake, and failed to grasp why she'd been putting in that amount of effort, until Zoe, with the intrinsic bluntness of petty bosses, told me, "His suffering can be cured. I can tell you the ten benefits of regular sex. If you marry him, you can live in our family manor." By "family manor", Madam Zoe meant a meadow and an unpainted ruin of a shack on the outskirts of the VIP strip.

"You'll finally be able to get out of that rotten one-room flat where, as far as I know, your grandparents died," Zoe added. "I also know that you sold their clothes. I mean their coats, and the new shoes you were supposed to put on the oldsters before you buried them."

How come a petty ministerial department head knew all about me?

"I've even heard you sold your grandmother's dentures and the Corega Fix Cream she used to glue them to her toothless gums," Zoe said.

She'd invited me for coffee and bought me a chocolate cake with walnuts and hazelnuts that cost a bomb. If I had been more observant, I would have realized immediately that she had paid about 60 levs — a financial outrage comparable to a fish swimming in sulfuric acid. Still, I felt that Zoe was in no position to ruin me. Since the day I was born, I'd looked like an absent-minded fool. They said Mom had then abandoned me to go off with a rich German, but the German guy suspected she was a bad egg and dumped her. Driven by this, Mom returned to collect me from the maternity ward. Perhaps that was the reason why my father harbored considerable doubts about whether I was or wasn't his daughter. He was in error, the poor devil. I was the spitting image of him, I'd inherited his freckles, his lies, and his uncouth ability to sense who was going to rip him apart — even before the scoundrel had talked to him.

I was a chip off the old block and I fell heir to his hunger for peace and solitude. When alone, you ruined yourself, no one else did it for you. I believed solitude was the garment we never took off. I had his freckles on my cheeks, and his foolish desire to be reckoned with — to be hated, to be scolded, yes, but never to go unnoticed, grey as a stained whisky glass forgotten on the shelf in a second-hand shop.

"I don't want to live with Fernanda in Spain without you," my father once said, and it seemed to me this was not one of his regular fibs. I knew he'd open his mouth to make me swallow another of his barefaced lies, but he would look at me peacefully, his eyes the brownish color of the leaves on the trees in the abandoned park where the junkies went to have a quiet drug binge. There, not far from the Struma River, three or four rusty swings jutted out, children played on them, while their mothers smoked and talked. I loved the kiddies, every one of them. Dark or light-skinned, they were dressed in clothes bought from second or perhaps fiftieth-hand stores; the sleeves looked so shiny and frayed as if a hundred tykes had already grown up in them — another reason I loved children.

I imagined what Nikolai the Magnificent looked like as a young boy.

I grew up with my mother's friends — smashing beauties all of them, each one looking for a rich gentleman, a real aristocrat capable of wresting them from the provincial abyss of grey apartment blocks. They hated the trampled gardens transformed into dried mud that still remembered the tires of the car that had last stuck in it. In the event that one of my mother's friends married a German citizen, I would go to be looked after by another of Mom's gal pals, but soon she too would find some fine nobleman. I packed up all my things in an old leather bag my father threw out after a rare surge of orderliness had gripped him.

I loved trash cans. In the evenings, ever since I could toddle and tell if a toy was good or torn, I discreetly went around the area where the dustbins were. I was usually in my best clothes; that way the citizens wouldn't suspect that such a pretty girl in a pink dress (that was why I hated the color pink) was after the garbage cans. I used to collect sensible discarded clothes, pieces of wire, and plastic crates, which I sold for ten, or twenty pennies at the Frog Market. All sorts of characters rambled around the shabby stalls there, but so did

Mom's sophisticated friends. I often begged them not to let her know that I'd hauled myself up to the Frog Market.

I came back home, my pockets heavy with clinking pennies. Maybe that was why I was early on the most brilliant kid in math in my class. By and large, I knew what the answer would be before Miss Dask had finished reading the math problem to us. I remember well, how could I forget? It all happened before my classmates knocked the hell out of me on account of my profound knowledge. One day, I turned to the teacher, "This problem is crystal clear! Why should they think we're so dumb?"

Everyone stared at the blackboard, and it seemed no student saw through the crystal clarity of the problem. Miss Dask didn't see any-thing either and said we were not dumb at all. During the break, my classmates covered my head with a coat. Most of them hit me on the skull. Some, I assumed they were boys, pinched my breasts, girls might have done that too, although at the time my tits were hardly bigger than erasers. In any case, I had since learned not to blubber. I had established that if you turned on the waterworks, you gave plea-sure to those who punched you in the face to prove you were not that smart.

I went home after school. For months, I'd been living tempo-rarily with one of my father's girlfriends, a fat, stingy woman who poured so little milk into my glass that from then on, every time I saw a fat woman, my stomach got instinctively tight with hunger. I think even my dad once took umbrage when they tossed me from a friend of his to one of Mom's gal pals, my old bag of shabby clothes accompanying me. It was the same bag my grandmother received as a valued present after she got married — my granny, the kindest person I'd known. She bathed and fed me the way all other kids were bathed and fed, and bought me a spoon of my own. I loved her for that. I love her even more now, even though she met her maker years ago. Grandmothers, I believe, turned the sky into a sunflower field, and I was sure Grandma had bought God a spoon of his own as well.

I wondered who my father had learned to lie so well from, having a mother like that. My granddad didn't lie either. On the contrary, if I lied to anybody, and I did lie because I believed I should, he would say, "Put your right hand up!" and after I did, he hit my knuckles with a wooden ruler. Then he'd make me calculate how many inches were 5.9 ft. I'd answer right away, even though my head could hardly reach the counter with his tools. He was a carpenter. Delighted by the meager mite's mathematical knowledge, grandfather forgot all about my fib-telling, took me to the Bee Sweetshop, and bought me the most expensive glass of apple juice and the biggest piece of cake at the confectionery. I ate slowly and gorged myself on chocolates because he wouldn't let me have anything sweet at home. Once I ate so much that I got sick and they took me by ambulance to the hospital in the town of Pernik. It was the first time I had heard Dad scold Grandpa, and it dawned on me — Dad didn't want me to die. I also found out why my dad didn't argue with people: if he had words with someone, he'd be caught out in a big fat lie.

So, my dad threw Grandma's leather bag in the dumpster, and bought me a suitcase in which I stored five pairs of knickers, five pairs of socks, two pairs of jeans, two blouses, a sweater, and five shirts — the best second-hand stuff I could lay my hands in my favorite Second Chance store. I also had one skirt, but it was so wide you could park a Mercedes in it. I regretted I couldn't wear the thing, so I used it as a pillowcase. That way, I saved Mom's friends the trouble of washing pillowcases. They thought I was a very sensible kid. Too bad I didn't have any luck whatsoever.

I immediately rushed to the dumpster to retrieve my leather bag, but my father — as he himself put it — could teach me a thing or two. That was to say, my grandmother must have been very sharp and smart when she gave birth to him, which is probably why his lies were so smooth you couldn't tell them from the truth. He caught me as I clutched my grandmother's bag and set the thing on fire in the garbage can. It was then that I ran a fever. Grandma looked at me from the world beyond as sadly as that cat — a neighbor threw away her kittens and set them on fire in the trash bin. I wanted to die — for the first and for the last time in my life — because I wanted to join Grandma in the world beyond. Even if she was in Hell, I'd somehow manage to solve the devil's math problems. I was sure of it. I was a smart one.

At that point, my father dropped one of the women he'd just begun to passionately love, and took me to the hospital. I thought he was going to leave me in the children's ward with Dr. Martina — she knew me, knew my threadworms and my bronchitis that kept on staying under my breastbone. Dr. Martina showed me what a sternum was. She knew my head lice, my red and white blood cells which I didn't know myself.

"These are little men in your blood that keep it alive, so you don't die," she had explained to me. I expected to see my wonderful Dr. Martina, but my father took me home, i.e. to his house. Apparently, he had bought a house and took care of me there until my temperature dropped, and the vanquished disease sniffed around my heels like a dog. No sooner had the vile fever gone down than I saw — Dad had bought me a new truly genuine leather bag.

"You're not going to cry, are you? Here's your bag."

I felt like shouting that he was the best father in the world, but how could I say this if he wasn't? I saw him rummage through a pile of Mom's discarded shoes and take the money I had collected after selling old clothes and things. He grabbed the crumpled five-lev bills I'd been hiding under his shirts that had gone out of style. I was flat broke, a kid as poor as the falcon that lived in my favorite fairytale Grandma often told me. He was a courageous bird but had no penny to bless himself with. Since then I started hiding money under the box of rat and mouse poison.

There were no mice or rats in Nikolai's house. No sparrow could sneak into the airspace of the property, and no ant could creep into the house. But I could. One of the bodyguards, Rosen, the young man allegedly suffering from a psychotic disorder, was Zoe's only son. Zoe had forked out sixty lev to treat me to a cup of coffee in the expensive Lilliput Cafe. There, an Egyptian served wonderful cakes.

"With my son Rosen, you can have a home of your own. I'll personally assist you to move your personal belongings to our family manor," she said. "It's a gorgeous place."

"Isn't Rosen a VIP area guard?" I asked.

I thought of the three eight-story tenement buildings in the North District, gray as the dark circles under Fernanda's eyes, Fernanda being my father's elderly wife (he'd sent me a clip. Fernanda looked 130, and the circles under her eyes were bigger than she was), but I didn't believe Dad, of course. Once in a blue moon, he sent me a hundred euros by way of apology for purloining my savings several years ago.

A boy in my class who I suspected had pinched my breasts the hardest after that simple math problem, would bring me a cup of tea and sell it to me at twenty cents off the price in the shop.

"Do you want me to solve math problems for you?" I asked him.

He shook his head. He spoke slowly, used swear words, and failing to heap a string of curses upon you was a sign he was happy. If you made him yell, you'd really gotten yourself into a fix. One day he brought me a cup of tea and sold it to me dirt cheap. He was as stingy as the gates of the VIP zone. A finch couldn't get through those five-barred barriers, so why would he sell me tea at a bargain price? It became clear why: the boy pressed me against the wall and kissed me. That is, bit me on the lip and squeezed my breasts if you could call that a kiss.

"I don't want this," I told him. I might as well have said, "I am thrilled to have you" as all my father's girlfriends without exception would have done inviting him into their hearts and purses. Dad uttered words and phrases softly and soothingly, which is why I have a suspicion that if someone was good at slick talking and used expressions like "I beg your pardon" and "Forgive me", he'd do the dirty on you.

"I don't want you to give me a discount!" I told my classmate. He was furious and kicked me, but not hard the way he kicked everyone else. I got the boot all right, but it was a careful and smooth one. On the following day, he brought me another cup of tea and didn't want me to pay him, but I refused to drink it. Since then I'd known that love was a discount store, and in it, they'd kick you for sure. The important thing was to know how to take a punch.

The only exception to this rule was Nikolai.

Zoe, our most note-worthy neighbor from the North district, a small-caliber chief at one of the numerous ministries, introduced me to her son, Rosen. He was tall, red-haired, and looked well-fed. If the guy didn't occasionally bark for no reason at all, you'd never have suspected that subtle mental affliction plagued him. A girlfriend of my father's, one of the many who had looked after me, had a dog, a huge mongrel called Storm. It was this mutt that taught me how to treat dogs. I tossed cheap sausage to him, and Storm soon fell in love with me. When Rosen started barking, I gave him a piece of steak his own mother Zoe had bought at my earnest request. After a couple of days, the woman invited me again to Lilliput Cafe. She forked out another fifty lev bill on cakes, which meant that I would probably have to marry Rosen. Consequently, I'd have to run away from Bulgaria to avoid marriage and save my skin, freckled and healthy as my father's.

It was because of my freckles that Dad was convinced I was his own flesh and blood, although he had declared to my mother, "The child is the flesh and blood of the neighbor from Entrance B, apartment 61." In this poky flat, lived a lonely professor of mathematics — Mom and a math professor, no way! But then how could you explain my mathematical genius, which earned me four consecutive thrashings? Once, my classmates smeared lipstick on the seat of my pants, then painted my hair and forehead green, using heat-resistant paint the school authorities intended to renovate the classroom doors with. I had another proof I was baked in the same clay as Dad.

"When I rest, I rust," he said every time he found a new love. My father, like me, sensed which person would ruin him: it was always my mother who did, so he ran away from her.

Zoe, who'd again shelled out fifty lev and ordered me a glass of Pina Colada, a slice of seed cake, and coffee at Lilliput Cafe, looked accusingly into my eyes, but I knew she couldn't ruin me. In this respect, I indeed was the spitting image of my father and suspected I wasn't Mom's child. Mom kept landing up in love with men who devastated her, and it was only on account of her knack for beating about the bush — after all, she was a graduate of the University of National and World Economy, Sofia — that Mom succeeded in adding quite a few thousand dollars more to her bank account after each hombre broke her heart.

I welcomed her ruination with open arms because after another thwarted love, she would take me to Deep Dish restaurant and buy me the most expensive steak in town, a glass of apple juice, and insisted that the waiter cut a fresh tomato salad for me in front of her eyes. She'd give me a pair of sneakers — either smaller or bigger than my size, but this was okay with me. I'd sell the pair at the Frog Market and buy sandals — almost as good as new — from the Second Chance store. She'd give me one of her blouses, too long and too big, but I wore it because I looked ugly in it, and no one pinched me. Solitude, an old friend of mine, whom I'd dubbed *the narrow shoe,* would join me. I was blissfully on my own, happy with the math problem book, and my textbooks in English, physics, and chemistry. Even the *German Grammar* tome on the table didn't bother me.

I let them believe I was slow on the uptake, a birdbrained chick cramming hard for her tests, a muddled brain. I didn't go to parties, didn't have a boyfriend, didn't drink, and didn't even smoke — crazy in the head that was all there was to it. Spending evenings in solitude did it. The textbooks were my friends. My father's sweethearts, even

Mom's Greek husband got a bit puzzled if they should care about me at all. I doubted it. Why should anyone worry about a weirdo? No reason at all. One day Dad said something quite without planning it. If he'd got a plan in mind, he'd positively walk around, a rosebud of a smile beaming on his face, his glance kissing the folks he met. This time, he didn't kiss anyone. He looked at me instead, his eyes as brown as a pile of leaves in the autumn a minute before the house-wife set them on fire.

"I wanted to become a history professor, my girl."

"Is that why your girlfriends are so scholarly?" I wanted to ask him, but didn't. He would have replied with the familiar rosebud on his face and another lie would've blossomed in our conversation. Unlike my father, Zoe was a boss of sorts and didn't have to lie to the riffraff in the North district, i.e. to us. Zoe had risen through the ranks, forcing many out of office, and saving her bacon. In Mom's opinion, it paid to comply with your superior. It meant you had to know when his birthday was, how his family celebrated Christmas, and when his child won the Spelling Bee in 2023. You could even invite your boss to your hotel room if need be — *we are only human after all*, Mom added. If one was the boss, we'd always be human, otherwise, why should we burn daylight?

"Eat," Zoe encouraged me, but even before I'd taken a bite of cake, she stood up. She was a tall woman with threateningly blonde hair who refused to tell me where she'd bought the dye from. The belle towered over me. We, humble residents of the three eight-story apartment buildings, knew that she frequented the most expensive gym in Sofia, the one affiliated with her important ministry. The ultimate goal was to cut a dashing figure. In my opinion,

Zoe squandered her money for nothing. She bent over to pick up her handbag and bumped into me. Maybe she'd planned to kiss me regally goodbye.

"He's stopped barking since he met you," Zoe breathed and gave me another kiss. "You did wonders. The psychiatrist from Heidelberg couldn't cure him. Professor Karov from the Bulgarian Psychiatric League couldn't either, but you, oh, I don't know what you did!" The woman discreetly — if waving a bundle of hundred lev bills under the noses of the loyal clientele of Lilliput Cafe could be described as "discretion" — stuffed the banknotes into my shirt pocket, right above my heart. "Now Rosen enters my room and kisses my hand. My own son kisses my hand three times a day!"

Mom's friend had a pooch that licked my hand three times a day if I gave him something to eat and a bone to gnaw on. Rosen, Zoe's son, worked as a guard for the VIP zone, an area as rigorously protected as the national gold reserve. Nikolai lived there.

Nikolai who claimed to be a poet visited our prestigious high school. Mr. Mikov, Our Bulgarian literature teacher, wrote sonnets I suspected were doggerel, doing us a service to remember him by. This pedagogue called Nikolai's work "poetry with a capital P" as did most of my classmates' parents who longed for excellent grades for their offspring. Two female educators held the same opinion and fell for Mikov. Fortunately, Miss Dimitrova, my math teacher, said there was as much poetry in Mr. Mikov's sonnets as there was gold in the trail of slime left by a snail. Our class teacher invited famous poets dubbed *his artistic colleagues*. They were expected to enrich our minds by reading their magnum opuses to us. I, as always, sat in the front of the classroom; where else would a dunce sit? There, the narrow shoe of solitude was light and comfortable. Occasionally, the boy who supplied me with tea, or some other stripling who'd offered me a sandwich at a discount would sit next to me, but I didn't have the hots for anybody.

Day in, day out, a girl gave me a few squares of chocolate, but I said "No" to her, so my classmates unanimously decided I was either underdeveloped or worse, I was asexual. One could easily explain why this had happened. Neither Mom nor Dad cared a fig about me, and I grew like a thistle in defiance of summer heat and winter blizzards. Some of my classmates' mothers sympathetically brought me hot soup on cold days, and I suspected my father had spent a lyrical hour or two with them as well. I didn't know that for sure, though. Our Bulgarian literature teacher invited poets — sons and daughters, proud heirs of distinguished parents, all living in the VIP zone. The dazzlingly white walls that surrounded the area looked like the dry bones of a prehistoric animal I'd seen at a museum. I gave up asking the teacher how come only scions of remarkable families wrote poems and essays, masterpieces every one of them. Go tell that to the Marines, pal.

I sat in the front row of tables in the classroom and listened as the representative of contemporary Bulgarian poetry or fiction read his masterwork. We were all eyes, careful not the miss the go-ahead sign our teacher gave us by lifting a thin booklet of Shakespeare's sonnets in the air. Bursts of deafening applause followed, and volcanic love for the poet or short story writer erupted straight from our hearts. That was the reason I hated modern literature as much as the whooping cough which knocked me down in winter.

On one of these occasions, Dad's girlfriend, under whose roof I happened to live at the time, rapidly sent me packing, and I landed in the hospital where Doc Martina worked. I knew the good woman's family name — Petrova. For days, I had nothing to do, so I read a couple of sonnets by the Bard of Avon. "*Shall I compare thee to a summer's day*?" God, wasn't it a miracle! How could that dumb teacher clutch Shakespeare's poetry book to squeeze applause out of his students? Hadn't the bigwigs' sons read Shakespeare's famous line "To be or not to be—-"? Not only did the big bananas write a pile of rubbish; they recited their fat poems, flaunting their disgrace!

It turned out Nikolai was one of these bards. I couldn't hear what he was reading. I could imagine Shakespeare's sonnets writhing as our teacher lifted the booklet in his fist.

Well, a great roar of applause broke out. Nikolai was looking at me. He was very handsome. I intensely disliked his poetry. It was a load of bunk, so I wondered why he should call it poetry in the first place. However, I liked him. It felt strange. For once in his life, my Dad must have forgotten that Mom was looking for a carrier rocket to launch her to a different space orbit far from the rust-covered fences and doors of North District. My dad was no gentleman. Far from it. He might have been once, but now he was a habitual liar with a freckled face. In case he really fell for Mom years ago, she must have appreciated his literature and poetry efforts. It didn't last long, though, less than nine months, until I was born. He was not averse to the idea of compensation because I, the child *he'd been raising*, might turn out not to be his own.

I grew quite fond of Nikolai - that is in my thoughts.

As a matter of fact, Rosen stopped suffering from the mental aberration that forced him to bark. He had begun to sing instead.

Come hell or high water, even though physics sought to prove hell didn't exist, Rosen did sing like an angel! He paid me ten bucks per minute to listen to him, but I refused to take his money. I truly loved his voice. It was huge, more powerful than the engines of the SUVs I'd seen plus those of the commoners' cars with plugged exhausts. His voice was as warm as the fur of the mongrel my mom's friend kept, and this creature was as beautiful as Nikolai. Every time I turned down the offer to pocket Rosen's money, he'd bark again. Nothing doing! I ended up accepting the bills and buying him a bar of chocolate. Rosen smiled happily like a baby on his first birthday or the way Dad grinned before he learned to spew another waterfall of his lies.

"I don't know why you don't want my money. It gives me the blues," Rosen drawled. His throat was a car that couldn't start and stopped in the middle of the street. "Why do you want to cut a hole in the hedge of the VIP area? Do you like hedges that much?

"Oh, I liked them even more than that," I told him.

From then on I started — leaf by leaf, twig by twig — cutting a hole in the hedge. In the beginning, thorns often broke off in my back and I asked my mother's stingy friend to help me get rid of them with her tweezers. She, of course, refused despite the fact I offered her Rosen's money. I went over to my dad's girlfriend who loved waifs and strays and kept the mongrel I happened to like. She said she was busy and told me to hop it. Finally, I went to — you could hardly guess who — the girl that day in, day out, offered me a few squares of chocolate. She accepted to treat the wounds on my back.

"You know where I'd like to touch you," she said.

"No," I snorted.

No matter what, she removed all deeply embedded barbs and

thorns, and I gained the impression she'd fished a whole hedge out of my back. The lassie carried out her work so thoroughly and conscientiously that the festering sores healed overnight. Clearly, I did not stay at the girl's apartment, although she offered me her savings, which amounted to 1,235 levs. From that day on, I squeezed through the hole in the hedge decked out in a leather jacket and leather trousers I'd bought for five levs from my beloved second-hand store.

"Why do you wear leather all the time?" Nikolai would ask me. "Why?"

I CUT THE LAST branch of the prickly hedge that separated me from Nikolai. Then I could not move. I could not catch my breath. I saw a meadow strewn with flowers so motley and brilliantly colored that my eyes hurt. The shades of pink alone were about a dozen; I counted that many in ten seconds. Assorted flowers were arranged in an endless row. Beside them, like scarlet ribbons, glowed a hundred thousand roses from deep red to salmon so pale as if someone spilled tea over them a week ago. A cloud of glorious blue flowers came into view, then purple, white, yellow, green, and orange: a gigantic garden of flowers that spilled down the banks of a majestic waterfall. I couldn't believe such a miracle could occur in our scruffy town. Rising to my feet, I wondered where the waterfall disgorged its waters, so I didn't notice a branch with thorns the size of sewing machine needles. They all poked holes in my neck.

I spotted it anyway — the water wasn't imprisoned in an Olympic-size swimming pool, not by a long shot. I saw a lake as blue as if a child had painted it in watercolors, its shores surrounded by flowers and trees whose names I didn't know. I caught sight of two beach umbrellas and three lounge chairs. A disturbing thought struck me: What are you up to now, Anna?

Against my better instincts, I didn't rush back to our North District, the ramshackle houses. I hated the asphalt street that was more a string of potholes than a road. They were on my mind, the grey, eight-story apartment buildings. Actually the walls had lost all color. Some flats had been spruced up as the proud owners tried to paint the plaster cheerfully yellow, while others, the careless type, deserted everything, leaving the rusty clotheslines to creak in the wind. I couldn't stand the balconies I'd been gazing at for years, most of them glassed. To me, they looked like old men wearing smudged glasses. I should have run away as fast as my legs would carry me from the paradise I'd landed in. I should've hidden in my one-room flat, which I had inherited from my grandparents.

It was Grandpa who met his maker first. He was a bricklayer and stonemason, and had a devil of a time with his job — I hoped there were devils somewhere, and I hoped they could hear me. The man used to read books my grandmother sprinkled with holy water. His favorites were *For Whom the Bell Tolls* and *The Old Man and the Sea*. If Grandfather had no time to read for a week, he ran a fever or was racked with severe knee pain, so excruciating he'd bite a piece of wood or the handle of a hammer to stop groaning. That was why Grandma sprinkled the books with holy water — to keep her man healthy, a simple guy who'd never lied to anybody.

"If you waste your time lying to folks," he used to tell her, "You won't be able to cut stone into pieces. Remember, the big houses you build are your footprints. Not your lies. Lies don't buy your only granddaughter the book about *The Wild Swan* and *Thumbelina.* You can't bring her new shoes from the Frog Market if you don't tell the truth."

God, I suppose you're very busy in heaven. You don't have time and you'll probably never look at my poky place, but, God, I'd like you to know what a good grandfather I had. Give him a dash of brandy in the evenings. He's somewhere near you, on the same cloud. You'll know it's him by the dust on his hands. A great man, my grandfather!

Grandpa would take me by the hand, and we would go shopping. I knew I shouldn't look at the expensive things because he'd buy them for me, and there'd be no money to fight against Grandma's high blood pressure. But sometimes — I didn't like the word "sometimes" very much, because it often happened to me — I'd steal a glance at the expensive cheese or the oranges, and Grandpa bought them. Then I couldn't look Grandma in her eyes. I wanted with all my skin, my bones, and the air I breathed in, to give her some of my healthy blood pressure, so at night I pressed my head against hers and didn't move for an hour. I believe an hour was the time my neck took to start hurting from pressing my forehead against hers. And yes, her blood pressure became as strong as Grandpa's brick hammer.

Grandma didn't lie to anybody because she had no time for nonsense. She cooked rice on Mondays, potatoes on Tuesdays, lentils on Wednesdays, and sorrel on Thursdays because they all had vitamins in them. I could see those vitamins bouncing around on my plate, and that was why I grew up a tall and nimble climber. On Sundays, we ate meatballs and bread. Those were the most delicious and happiest meatballs in town. Unfortunately, Grandfather stopped reading *For Whom the Bell Tolls.* He didn't read his book for three days, and although Grandma sprinkled holy water on its front cover, he died on the fourth day. Grandma and I could barely lift him up to wash him and dress him. We buried him in the oldest suit because the old man was on his way to God, and God was a hard worker, a stone-mason like Grandpa, and didn't wear designer suits. He had built all the stones, the land, the water, and everything else in the world, so they were colleagues, those two, and God would give Grandpa heavy-duty work clothes.

Grandma said that to die meant to become a clump of grass, so you should not trample grass underfoot — you didn't know who you could be stepping on. Grandma said that we, the human beings, were the clocks of God. If there were no people, time would dry up and wouldn't move forward. It would simply evaporate. It was by looking after our life that God measured how much time had passed, Grandma added. When a man or a woman died, one of God's clocks stopped, and time became smaller. "You have to know, Anna — as many people, as many times, and as many timepieces our good God has."

Those words of hers gave me a reason to believe that my father had learned to lie from Grandma. He told his whoppers with such consummate skill that I wondered how much was fabricated and how much was the truth. I could tell he was fibbing by his smiles made of gold. Nothing tricked you into doing stupid things more than gold. Gold made man plant flowers that commoners had never seen — pink, red, yellow, and purple. Gold gave you a water-fall that licked at the icy lake as blue as a watercolor painting of a child. Behind the fence tall as a tower crane, a hundred yards away, the apartment buildings jutted out. Folks were glad to have a poky bachelor flat with a glassed-in balcony. My father didn't tell a lie for hours, even for the entire morning if the previous night he had read about Grandpa's tolling bell or Grandpa's book about the old man and his sea.

"Hemingway's mad," my father would hint, and I thought Hemingway was the guy who'd taken him to the cleaners in a poker game. Maybe I was wrong. Maybe this chap Hemingway was a bricklayer or a stonemason like Grandpa and like God, but my father cut me short. "Mind your own business, you fool. Go peel potatoes."

Mom left my father for her Dutch husband and Dad got himself a girlfriend, a literature teacher — he loved teachers for their generosity. I strongly suspected literature had to do with thick books like Grandpa's *Bell*, and the teacher in question one day said to me, "Hemingway was not a bricklayer. He was a writer."

So far, so good. As long as Grandpa liked *For Whom the Bell Tolls* and Dad didn't lie for hours on account of Hemingway, I jumped to the conclusion this guy wasn't a thief. I was six. The literature teacher and Dad took me to a seaside resort. When I saw the sea, I gasped, "Good Lord, it's great that you provided so much water, and it's even better you got the old man to write something about it." When I first caught a glimpse of the lake shimmering on Nikolai's giant lawn, I thought about the old man and his boat. Too bad Hemingway wasn't here to describe the blue expanse and the flowers surrounding it.

"Don't run away. If you do, you admit they buried you in the mud and they're pissing on your head," my father would say to me on the rare mornings when he wasn't lying because he had read something about the sea again. "Don't give in. Yes, they've clouted you one, but you're sure your neck is not broken yet."

It was a pity my father ditched the teacher who had told me the truth about writers. She couldn't stand a liar, and must have picked up the habit because of teaching literature. I'd come to believe that a book could not tolerate a lie. It died if you pushed fabrications into its pages, even though they gave you a fat literary prize for it. The woman said my father's lies exacerbated her insomnia. My father did his best to reassure her and hinted he could make love more often that way, but she snapped, "Love, like literature, does not tolerate lies," and that was all there was to it.

"All right," my father agreed as he gathered his clothes, toothbrush, and shaving cream. Within a quarter of an hour, he moved out of her apartment. The teacher sobbed for a while. I gave her a glass of water, and she hugged me, weeping copious tears that soiled my comparatively new T-shirt. I forgave her because she took me for a walk in the park and regaled me with a tale about a white whale called Moby Dick. To cut a long story short, the woman didn't give me any money before she went away. I didn't have a penny to bless myself with.

"There are no white whales," I told her. Obviously, she had embraced my father's lies with both arms.

Go ahead, let them slap you across the face. You can live with that, but you know they haven't buried you in the mud, I said to myself. Rosen, Zoe's son (and Zoe was a boss at one of the numerous ministries in Sofia) barked no more. Instead, he fell into the habit of kissing both my and his mother's hands. On a cigarette pack, the young man had drawn the marble path the window of Nikolai's room gave a view of.

"You need to climb over here," the red-haired giant explained to me. "Here, on that terrace, see? It's easy. They make the housemaid sweep the damned thing every morning. Then you have to squeak through the bathroom window. You're as thin as my old belt, you'll do the trick all right. But why do you want to sneak up on Nikolai? He's skinny. He can't do the job you want him to do. I can. He can't hold a candle to me, I tell you. If you marry me… Mom has promised, she'll give me the house and the backyard. I'll look after you. But one thing worries me, you know."

Rosen spoke at length in a thick voice God himself must have hammered out for him at His forge. Poor Rosen had no one to talk to. No living soul would listen to him, and maybe that was the reason he had started to bark. When I was at his side, he sang or prattled away, my face under siege of his blue eyes as brilliant as a liquor bottle. He'd grab my hand and put it on his forehead.

"You make my headache go away," he explained. "I put it where it hurts and the pain wears off." After a while, he burst into song.

"There's a bad part to it," the redhead continued. "Mom thinks we've been doing the job, Nikolai and me. She thinks Nikolai pays me, but he doesn't. He goes and says a silly thing. 'If you put your fingers there,' he says, 'It doesn't hurt anymore. It's bad now. It hurts so much I can't talk.' He points to the place where the pain digs into him and puts my hand there. Mom thinks I've done wrong. But I haven't. I want you. I'd do it for you. All day long I will. Or I'll sing to you. It's great you're listening to me, Anna. If you want, I'll give you two hundred bucks, and we can get married."

"How can I climb up onto Nikolai's terrace?" I asked. Rosen's shoulders looked like mountains, and his fingers could grind bull's bones into powder.

"There's no need to climb," he assured me. "I'll lift you up. You're as light as a paperclip. I can lift you with one hand. Here's where my chest hurts. Put your hand on it, Anna. It feels good! Nobody's gonna do the job for you like me. Do you want me? I have two hundred bucks. Let's get married. What's Nikolai got to do with it? I've no idea what you're prattling on about, Anna. What poetry? Poetry means you're not all there. Stop it! All right then, if it's poetry you want, go get Nikolai to read you crap, you dunderhead. Mom will give us the house, she'll transfer the property to me. I tell you. All right, call me after you squeeze through the hole in the hedge. I'll come and lift you up onto Nikolai's terrace."

The day before I cut the last branch and destroyed the last biting thistle, I went to see Rosen.

"Please sing to me," I said.

God, I know you are too busy to come visit me. I guess there's no way you can hear me, but please, God, help Rosen get well soon. Let him be a normal being like you and me. Make him feel happy at least once a year. Find him some other girl, God. Don't give him to me. I'm a nonstandard lass raised by my dad's girlfriends and my mom's husbands. I can't stay long with anyone and I can't lie to anybody.

Sometimes I love Dad and his old man and the sea, but I hate fib-telling, and I've learned the hard way to keep mum. If I lied to somebody, I stuck a pin in my own tongue. I didn't want to read *The Old Man and the Sea* so I didn't fabricate stories in the morning, God. Let me grow up alone, grow old alone, and die alone. Don't let me, like my father, ditch literature teachers who hated lies. Let me not have husbands who got diabetes like Mom's men did when she left them for someone else. If I lived alone, God, I wouldn't dump anyone. Literature teachers would talk about the old man and the sea for years and would repeat the little white lie about the white whale.

Guys wouldn't get diabetes, they'd have children and take them to seaside resorts. They'd buy the little ones expensive things, but not too often, and they'd have enough money to quickly lower their wives' high blood pressure. I hoped the fathers would take their kids to Cape Kaliakra at the Black Sea coast in Bulgaria. There, the tykes would see with their own eyes what a great hand at making worlds you are, God. They'd know you had made seas out of the water, and you gave the seas fish, fishermen, boats, ships, and sails. Give Rosen another girl, God, don't give me to him.

Grandma lived three years longer than Grandpa. These were my happiest years. We planted strawberries together. She taught me to keep down weeds, showed me how to graft trees using five different techniques, and explained to me which wild apple seedlings could marry red delicious apple and raise its child, the scion wood that would produce new shoots and the desired fruit. The scion would become the only son of the hardy wild tree. Grandma taught me to read and, on her meager pension, she bought me the most expensive picture book about the wildest swans in Denmark.

"I'm going to die soon," she told me. "Don't you be afraid, girl! I'll become grass. If you want, I will grow in the pot over there, so you won't be alone. To be honest, Anna, you'd better remain alone, for you won't find a man like your grandfather. Our Lord only makes such a guy once, and then, though he is our God — I've never denied that He made the seas, the sledgehammers, and the stones — He wouldn't carve a man as good as your grandfather for the second time. It's because all justice and goodness went to Grandpa, and now I know that he is grass. Anna, I'll be grass, too. Our roots will be warm and snug together in the winter.

Maybe your grandpa is the shadow of this house. Then I will become a shadow of a shack. When the sun goes down, I'll inch my way toward him. We, two flickering shadows, will weigh no one down, sweetie, we will only protect you from the summer heat. When I get to your grandpa, we'll hug each other. You should know, sweetheart, that if one shadow leans towards another, it's me and your grandpa. Come and glance at us sometimes.

Grandma passed away. My father didn't come to the funeral and didn't see her off on the road to the sunset. He was on holiday in Spain with a new girlfriend, the wealthy daughter of a prominent businessman. She could have made a good translator, this exceptional daughter if she wasn't so rich. I thought a girl translated well if she had no money; that was why she left a piece of Bulgaria in the words another person had written. And if not, then why bother?

Writing a book was as easy as falling off a log. And it was fun, too. You didn't know where the characters wanted to go, so you followed in their footsteps. A book was solitude, a narrow shoe that pinched and told you that you were still breathing. It was somebody else's shadow that looked for the kiss on your lips. My father's translator was rolling in dough and asked Dad to go on vacation with her to interesting cities all over Europe. The woman said she'd like to buy me a cup of coffee at the local café in Saragossa which was also in Europe. She insisted it was not a waste of time to translate a novel; however, it was much more pleasant to visit great places accompanied by a great man, my father.

"Besides," she added, "Your dad is not fussy. He doesn't get mad when he's not wearing a Ralph Lauren polo shirt. And he's fit, I assure you."

It was because of this literary translator that my father failed to come and bathe Grandma after she peacefully met her maker. It was not her ailments — her upset stomach, stiffness, or joint pain — that did it. Grandma would take a nap, an hour or two in the afternoon, when, in her opinion, Our Lord also lay dozing so that He'd be strong enough to do more good things for people. Grandma would wake up at 3 pm, and we'd fix something to eat, a big afternoon snack, which was also our dinner and breakfast on the following day. We loved to make pancakes. That day we had many eggs, so we were two well-to-do ladies. It was half past three and Grandma didn't wake up. At a quarter past four, she was still sleeping. At five o'clock, I knew something had gone wrong.

"Grandma, grandma, let's go cook pancakes!" I said as I lightly tapped her on the shoulder. She didn't move, nor did she say any-thing or wave her hand. She didn't smile. She had a rule not to smile at you before she put on her dentures. To be honest, she was very beautiful to me.

"Get up, Grandma."

She didn't get up. I glanced at that pot — grass grew in it, strong as the summer wind, beautiful as the ring of that literature teacher who couldn't stand lies, warm as the cries of a newborn baby. I believed there was nothing as strong as a girl born to a father who lied from dawn to midnight and only once a month, twice at most, did he speak the truth because he'd read a page or two from the book about that old man and the sea.

Grandma was dead.

The shadow of the apartment building slowly leaned toward our one-room flat. I knew Grandma was already making soup, God and

Grandpa had been cutting stones for hours together, and they were both very hungry. But Grandma wouldn't bring them the soup bowls right away. She would first give Grandpa a glass of brandy, then she'd sprinkle The *Old Man and the Sea* with holy water so that her man would be as hard as the stones he cut, and then — she did this rarely, thinking I wasn't watching — the old woman would wipe Grandfather's forehead with a shabby towel.

The shadow of the apartment building touched the shadow our block of flats had cast on the street. Was Grandma giving Grandpa a new coat to put on, or was she still wiping the sweat from his forehead with that towel?

I couldn't lift her up. I asked our neighbor to help me, but he was busy. I called my dad's girlfriend, the last-but-one of his belles, but she, too, could not assist me, "owing to a previous engagement". I ran to the house of the teacher who hated lies, but I saw a copy of her obituary in the Telegraph stuck on the front door. No way.

I washed Grandma myself. I cut her nightgown with her scissors and used the big pieces of cloth to clean up the spilled water after I bathed her. I chose her best socks to put on her feet. It took me an hour — or was it one hundred hours — to dress her up in her most expensive blouse. I knew I could get five bucks for that outfit at the Frog Market, but Grandma had to join the grass decked out in her Sunday best. I left her skirts in her coffin — she only had two. I tucked the black one under her legs, wrapped the blue one around her, and tied it with a string.

I gave our neighbor the TV, which he swapped for a bottle of brandy, and the two of us, the middle-aged man and I, buried her. I told the priest I had no money to pay for the burial service, so he took our fridge. That was how I inherited Grandma's one-room flat.

I didn't have a fridge or a TV, but I slept in her bed. I sold mine at the Frog Market for six levs and fifty cents. How nice it was to keep dreaming about Grandma in her bed.

Every night the shadow of the gray apartment building caressed the dark windows of ours, and that grass in the pot, impatient as a baby's cries, grew thicker. I wished then — and only then — that I was a woman like other women, that I had a daughter, and that my daughter had a baby girl. No one could love that child more than me. I would become grass for the little one to play on, and I'd always be green. Always.

Maybe my grandmother had turned into a grasshopper.

—∾—

"ONCE YOU PUT A grasshopper in a cage, it dies," Grandma once said. "Never weave a grasshopper's cage, my girl. If I don't become a clump of grass, I'll be a grasshopper. I'll jump and I'll run."

I took Rosen, who had long since stopped barking, to Grandma's grave. There he sang to her. Yoan Kukuzel, the first Bulgarian composer of the 12th century CE, dubbed the Angel-Voiced by renowned historians, would have lost ten pounds or melted away had he heard Rosen's voice. Poor, poor Kukuzel! Despite his fame, couldn't hold a candle to the big man.

"You're a genius," I told Rosen, but he didn't know what that word meant and got offended.

"I can do that job!" he blurted out in a voice that made stones tremble ten feet underground. "I'm not what you think I am. Let me show you. Here and now!"

I didn't have to call Rosen after I was struck all of a heap the minute I glimpsed the huge flowers by the lake.

"Are you gaping at the peonies?" he asked me. "Twenty-five gardeners toil and moil here, watering, digging, and weeding them. Don't tell me to shut up. I'll speak as long as I want, Anna. There's nobody at their place. Nikolai's mother is in Paris, his father's vanished into thin air. I'm not sure if Nikolai's flown the coop or not. To make a long story short, he'll be back soon because he asked me not to go back home. 'It hurts me,' he says, and I'll have to put my hands on him until he gets over it. He told me, 'You possess extrasensory perception.' Perception my ass. He's paying me two grand per minute, not bad, eh? I'll give you five grand. Will you marry me?"

Rosen lifted me up to the terrace.

I squeezed through the bathroom window.

"I left it open for you," he shouted.

You could ride a horse on that terrace. But where on earth would you find one? Horses and cattle died out a long time ago. You couldn't even find a horseshoe.

If you wanted, you could ride an all-terrain vehicle here. I had no idea what they called the stone tiles that made my buttocks tingle — marble, granite, quartz… I got an A in chemistry. In any case, here the stones were bluish, translucent as the water in the sea, and warm to the touch. A special terrace. Lots of flower pots, roses, and various plants in glass bowls. The door to the room was massive, light yellowish–brown, and I asked myself how it was possible for an elegant door to be both wooden and transparent at the same time. A little window was left open. Come off it. It wasn't a window, it was an opening made in the fortified wall where you could deploy firearms.

So far, so good. It was nothing but a hole. Even if this hole had been punched in a diamond, I'd slip through it.

I was about to muck up my beautiful plan. I failed to muscle my way through the window, so I had to push the smallest flower pot under it. I stepped on the edge of the pot, careful not to stomp on the flower. An age passed and in the end, I managed to clamber up the wall. Then I hung upside down, my head almost hitting the bathtub. The truth was the thing wasn't exactly a bathtub, it was an aquarium where you could accommodate a whale.

I didn't care for bathtubs. I never had. In our one-room flat, the water heater ran once a week for an hour. We were often short of cash, couldn't sell a thing at the Frog Market, and we could afford the water heater once a month, or didn't use the thing at all. Summer was a horse of a different color, as my father used to say. In July, Grandma and I put buckets of water on the windowsill and waited for the water to heat up. Then we thoroughly scrubbed up and washed our hair every single day.

My breath solidified in my lungs, and my back stiffened up as I saw Nikolai's room. Out of nowhere, I remembered what my father said one day when he didn't hate the whole world, "If they incapacitate you and you cannot make a move, it is a forgivable mistake to pee in your pants. Count to five slowly then get up. Kick their asses. You are Herr von Eustatius's daughter, i.e. my immediate descendant, Anna. Get up!"

Everything in the room was beautiful yellowish wood, including the life-size nude male statue. There was no bed. Something resembling a mattress, so clean that its immaculacy caused shimmering in your vision, took up one-third of the huge floor area. A dozen books lay on the mattress. The volumes were all written by the same author, Nikolai Caramelitev, i.e. Nikolai I'd been dreaming of. His colored photograph, beautiful as a snowdrop in early spring, stared at me from the ceiling. Nikolai Caramelitev looked magnificent and had obviously penned many novels. I hid behind the statue of the handsome young man and waited. The afternoon wore on, the air in the room smelled of sweet-scented flowers, and the statue of the teenager looked so energetic and full of life as if he was going to kick me in the ankle any minute now. I kept on waiting. I had patience similar to what the sea God had made would look like a cup of decaf coffee.

I am an English teacher, a serious one, and I believe an attractive woman.

A lot of people have been doing it lately, and I'd called them cowards, even mean rats, but there is logic in the world, and I'm a logical person. How about this: someone has pestered you, ground you down, and forced you to kiss the shoes of the man you're in love with while she's making love or maybe making death to him before your very eyes. The important lady wants you to be sure what exactly she's doing.

She has bodyguards and money to burn. She is influential. What will you do then? You cannot kill her. Whatever you do they'll call you a freak and a criminal. If you try to prove she is guilty, the malefactor will pay whomever she has to, so, if you don't die in a hospital, you'll surely cash in your chips after the hospital discharges you. The only thing you could resort to would be me to smile obsequiously at Madam whose guts you hate.

"Be happy with this wonderful man, God bless you," you'd whisper in her ear. "My dear friend, it is a pity you don't know something about that man — his partner, they tell me in full confidence, caught *that disease* just from physical contact." But you might not say so because you're as old-fashioned as an ancient pair of pants. This man still means heaven, land, food, and water to you. You could, of course, put a couple of stones in your pocket, as Virginia Woolf, the famous writer, did, and drown yourself in any sufficiently deep body of water.

You have to make up your mind. I just offer a way out.

If you're smart, you pay one hundred and seventy levs and put your own obituary in *The Telegraph* national newspaper. It is advisable to stick the text of the obituary on your own apartment door. If the blood in your arteries is capable of boiling, calm it down — because after a woman pushes up the daisies everyone remembers only her dastardly deeds. Therefore, lady, you'd better hide somewhere and observe how your acquaintances will react to the news of your death. Take neat notes on who looks sad, and who's grinning with joy that you've kicked the bucket.

However, the saddest thing happens if no one looks at your obituary and your departure is not announced with much fanfare. So what! You refuse to come back to the trampled garden, the one–room flat where the toilet keeps clogging, and the stink of cockroach killer dominates the entire apartment building. You go on living simply because Herr von Eustatius has whispered to you, "Look at the shadow the block of flats casts, the one over there. Can you see it? It is impatient, this shadow is. It's rushing to touch the house next door. That's how I run towards you, my dearest. Always think of me as a shadow that loves you."

I'm an English teacher that has missed the biggest chances in life. She despises the students who yell and shout at her, she is ashamed of the plagiarized term papers and hates them. The poor thing lives with the evenings of dull soap operas, but then lo and behold! Eustatius comes in. Eustatius brings her flowers and whispers in her ear: "Love is not love which alters when it alteration finds" her favorite Sonnet 116 by Shakespeare. No one has ever done that before. Eustatius…

"Your comfortable flat is my quiet harbor, sweetheart. You transform my days into a citadel of serenity, a glow of happiness I've felt so rarely," he continues, sotto voce.

I used to be an English teacher, a serious one.

Now, you are a miracle, I say to myself.

In the evenings, you cook Bulgarian Hot Chicken, his favorite meal, you get up an hour earlier in the morning to iron his shirts while his ham and cheese sandwiches sizzle on the grill. Sometimes he brings a bundle, lots and lots of money, because he plays poker and does it brilliantly. There are days when stress mounts, he looks at you sadly and you kiss him, his tears dying on your lips. He writes poems for you and leaves the tiny sheets of paper in the pocket of your most expensive jacket, which you, like any other perspicacious Bulgarian, bought from the second-hand shop. On a number of occasions, he hides the fiery stanzas among your underpants and dedicates them to your skin, which no one has cared to notice before. He kisses your hand, which you think is too rough and work-worn. Your fingernails have never looked good, but his kisses blossom on each finger individually.

"You are my blessing," he says to your thumb. "You are my weakness," to the index finger.

I'm just a woman who has moved from a small village to Sofia, the capital of Bulgaria. The simple village girl falls victim to a love affair in her sophomore year of university. The man she dates turns out to be married. She doesn't let her bitter disappointment show.

Eustatius…

"Will you take care of my daughter?" he once asked. "I love you because you …because I feel you will be a good mother to her."

…..And in the midst of passion — don't I hate the shallow noun "*passion*", the yellow ingredient of the crushingly weak novels I read! I'm just a — let me admit it — a spinster ashamed of dirty words. Let me acknowledge the existence of a fact: intimate companionship used to scare me and to get over my qualms, I read those dull books about single ladies. I feel embarrassed that I've perused every word of these tomes. However, I pride myself on having pored over everything translated into Bulgarian by Gabriel Garcia Marquez, Hemingway, Brodsky, etc.

Life isn't a short story by Fitzgerald, it is a grey apartment building and three hundred levs to stretch until payday in three weeks, plus your old cousin you have to take to the endocrinologist. Someone will quite accidentally hit you with their car, the windows of your flat will end up broken, or as luck would have it, someone will carve the phrase "dirty bitch" on your front door. You cannot guess who that someone is because you've given bad marks to eleven students. They have not heard a word about present perfect continuous and past perfect continuous tenses, but the parents are convinced that their "little one" knows everything there is to know about English grammar. It goes without saying that the 'child' speaks English perfectly.

"Will you be her mother?" Eustatius asks me. He's been asking me that question for a month now. Loneliness has taught me to carefully count the pennies in my purse, to remember exactly how many times a guy has insulted me, excluding the phrase "dirty bitch". That's my nickname, and I'm sure they've used it a billion times already. I once decided to buy ten bottles of rose oil — it cures the itchy rash which comes out on my belly when I am called something dirtier than "dirty bitch". I paid for the rose oil and when I counted the bottles at home, it turned out there were nine in the box. One costs fifty-five levs.

"I'll try to be a mother to her," I assured Eustatius.

"She's a very lonely girl," he murmured. "I was even told — of course, it may not be true — that she was in love with a classmate, a lass."

Just my luck! Obviously, this mademoiselle will be a thorn in my side.

"She's always been special. She listened while I was having words with her mother. Every time her mom found a new boyfriend, my daughter would have no food for days, and when I — you see, my beautiful dark-eyed love — I was not made to be lonely, spiritually or bodily. I tried to find a soul mate, and the child kept on losing weight. She's called Anna, I named my daughter Anna! At times, she became so weak she couldn't get out of bed. I was very sorry for her. I looked at her and I felt sick. My chest hurt..."

In those moments, Eustatius's face looked thin and haggard. I massaged his body gently, and beautifully, the way I had dreamed of touching a man all my life, but Eustatius was much more than a dream to me. He was an ocean, and my dream was a lonely sunset over the waves.

To me, Eustatius was more precious than all the books written by the finest, bravest, and most brilliant minds of mankind. My dreams were a tiny dash in one of these great works. That was what Eustatius was to me. I was ready to use my modest salary to buy things for his daughter, and the other girl she was in love with. I was ready to sell the small house in the village of Drugan that my father and mother, may their souls rest in peace, had left me. Then I would have enough money to cook chicken soup for Anna almost every day. She was thin, Eustatius told me. Surely her hemoglobin was low. After the death of Anna's grandparents, Eustatius's dear mother and father, the girl didn't have a dime to her name. Alas, she was short on cash all the time. He, Eustatius, sent her some money when he won at poker, but you could rely on poker as much as you relied on the stormy winds — that is, not at all.

"Will you take care of her after I go away?"

I'd jump into a bathtub of boiling quicksilver if Eustatius ask me to. I answered him firmly, "Of course."

Never has love been so deep, so beautiful, and passionate as it was that night. When I think about it now, I realize that maybe Eustatius made me so happy out of gratitude for my warm heart. What do writers of sappy romance novels know about life? How flat, nonsensical, and hollow their tomes sound. Everything about Eustatius was beautiful. Every word he uttered was magic, every square inch of his body was a miracle. God, why didn't you ask him to write down every sentence he had whispered to me? With him, I knew I was beautiful, I could have anyone I wanted, but after Eustatius, could I want anyone? Could I really?

"She will come to your place tomorrow," he said.

She did. Eustatius's daughter was as thin as a scarecrow, a walking pair of scissors, her hair the color of car tires. Why should my memories of the wonderful metaphors woven by Federico Garcia Lorca, my favorite poet, betray me? I could not offer his daughter a gentle word. She wore the ugliest clothes one could buy at the Second-hand store in Levski Square. I knew that for a fact because I, like everybody else in the neighborhood, shopped there. Once every three months they put out interesting clothes; you buy T-shirts for a buck or you could make a combination: three shirts, one pair of jeans, and a jacket. And you pay two levs. However, those were T-shirts that only a suicidal character would wear. That was what Eustatius' daughter was — a complete nutcase. I didn't like her at all.

"Good evening," I said to her. "How are you?"

She answered nothing, nor did she deign to look up as she sneaked past me like a stink of burning rubber. Though I'd most hospitably let her live under my roof, the young grass snake wouldn't talk to me. All the time, she kept mum in my presence as if I were a toilet brush. All I could think of was that she walked too cautiously. Her footsteps made me think of a criminal or a beggar who rummaged through bins late at night to collect things that appeared still usable. Then she ran straight to the kitchen stove. The young reptile had never coiled herself in my studio apartment before. I could smell the disgusting second-hand shop stink that drifted up from her jacket.

She'd open the oven and pull out the whole dish. I only had 129 bucks before the next payday. Fourteen hungry days stared me in the face, but I bought — from the most expensive butcher's shop, mind you — some nice pork, the kind I could afford at Christmas or on my birthday. My birthdays are beautiful and lonely. I bought coffee for my two friends from college, the first one a spinster, and the other a happily divorced gal. I prepared delicious roast beef in the evening and ate it for a week. I could give myself this tiny bit of pleasure because I cooked well. My grateful thanks went to God, whom some intellectuals called "the universe". I met Eustatius and cooked grilled pigeons for him, strictly following my dear grandmother's recipe. I gave him braised sausages with onion gravy, cabbage, and chicken nuggets.

The happiest moments in my life… I dreamed of melting under Eustatius's gaze. Watching him eat the tasty dish I'd prepared for him was sheer bliss. I borrowed money from my two friends, yes, I did, for I had realized the universe had an intriguing plan for me. I was not the engine of an old jalopy that had worked faithfully for its owner for thirty years. Let someone else languish in a classroom filled with big-headed students who could spell correctly only a dozen swear words. (I hate the adjective "dirty" so I avoid using it.) I was born to cook superb food for Eustatius. This, and only this, was my calling.

His daughter was disgusting. On the second day of her stay under my roof, she took out the whole platter with the expensive pork. I'd spent an hour picking and choosing the best and the freshest piece of meat, and I paid fifty levs for it! She left the platter in the sink and forgot to wash her hands. Then the young jellyfish buried her fingers in the stew, grabbed the chunk of meat that cost fifty bucks, and bit into it. Gravy dripped down her chin and thumbs. Grease stains gleamed on the sleeves of her filthy shirt. The jellyfish had dropped blobs of sauce on the tiles in my kitchenette. If I had admired anything early in life, it was cleanliness and order. Not a speck of dust spoiled the perfection of my clean sheets. The floor of my studio apartment, spotless and impeccable, reflected my image like a mirror. But sauce erupted from the chick's (i.e. Eustatius's daughter) lips — and dripped on the floor. She took no heed. The adolescent jellyfish grabbed another piece of meat and stuffed it into her mouth, although she hadn't swallowed the last one yet. Then she shoveled down a big potato. I thought the medusa was going to choke on a bone, and handed her a glass of water, but she pushed me rudely as if I had scarlet fever or COVID-19.

She gobbled down all the meat. I couldn't say exactly how many minutes it took the young reptile to devour everything she could lay her hands on, although I am a person who values accuracy and precision. Might have been seven minutes, or even five. Once the meat was gone, the girl picked up the platter and drank the sauce straight from it. I still marvel to this day how the jellyfish did it — may the Universe forgive me — I prayed that she would choke to death and fall down breathless on my kitchen floor, a surface she had brutally vandalized. The gravy must have still been very hot because occasionally she opened her mouth the way a dump truck lifted up its dump bed. She swilled the sauce, but even that wasn't good enough for her. She licked the platter clean, then caught sight of the caramel custard I'd prepared. I'd selected four eggs — buy one get one free, the salesperson informed me, the kind guy he was. The eggs were small really, but still within their expiration date marked on the label. The jellyfish chucked the platter down on the windowsill next to my flowers — I found intense pleasure in looking at their exquisite petals — Kalanchoe, violets, pansies that were all magnificent!

Eustatius's daughter grabbed the first caramel custard bowl and rapidly guzzled it down. She wolfed down the second one too. Then the reptile put her head under the faucet and started guzzling water directly from the tap. It was true my glasses were not exemplary; could one buy nice glasses from a second-hand store? No, sir. But they were decent second-hand glasses, indeed. The jellyfish could have poured water into one. Then, in her shabby clothes that were 20 cents apiece, she slumped onto my sofa as if a butcher had cut off her head. This piece of furniture was beautiful. My lovely grandmother, God rest her soul, had made the quilt it was covered with. The quilt had been in use for more than fifty years, 52 to be precise. It glistened, sparkling clean and soft. Eustatius's daughter, her sneakers caked with dust and she, covered in stains all over the place, sprawled out on my sofa — on which my dear mother slept before she went to her glory. I kept it as a memento of my time with Mom. How happy we were at Christmas, my dear mother and I! How magnificently the Bengal fire sparkled. My mother, the saint!

"Martha, be careful, sweetie! Get yourself a decent man. I pray to God to send him your way, my dear child. There is no greater joy in a lady's life than a man, little Martha!" She could not fulfill her deepest wish to see me in love with a solid guy, but lo and behold — it came true! My mother was right about everything. There had never been, and would never be, a greater joy for me — Eustatius. My Eustatius!

But his daughter… that hideous creature. That insolent hyena!

Why didn't I think about what Eustatius said? "*Thou wilt keep her in perfect peace.*" Yes, I am sure it was the poet's subtle way of saying goodbye to me. Because he loved me. He adored every square inch of my skin, to which he dedicated a beautiful poem and sealed it with a kiss. Nothing compared to Eustatius. "*You will take care of her,*" he had whispered. "*Won't you?*"

I thought he'd come back home sad as always after losing badly at poker — one could trust a poker game as much as the croaking frogs in the river — however, my lingering kisses erased his sadness. I let him lie in a hot bubble bath. The universe had not given me a child, but I had Eustatius. I was jubilant at the touch of his fingers. His quiet breathing made me happy. I was truly blessed. That evening, he didn't come home like he did every other day. I waited for him from 6 pm until 10 am the following day. I was devastated, I was terrified — his clothes were gone, his socks were gone, his shoes were gone.

My only coat, which had not been bought from the second-hand store at the intersection of Levski Street and Summer Avenue, was also gone. I knew what had happened — he was left penniless. He could sell my coat for fifty levs, although I forked out 1782 levs for it in honor of my fortieth birthday. I passionately hoped Eustatius could sell the thing for more than thirty levs. Fifty-five or even sixty? Why didn't it cross my mind that when he asked me, "Will you take care of her?" he was actually saying goodbye, my love? The infinite temptation of Eustatius's farewell... What could I do, a teacher who worked with recalcitrant students devoid of any desire to open a popular novel, let alone a literature textbook?

His daughter was asleep in the kitchenette. I had a nice pair of jeans that cost seven bucks in the Second Chance store, and I'd bought a second pair for fifteen levs. Without asking me, the jellyfish had put on one of my blue shirts and my jacket from the Second Chance that had cost twelve levs apiece, and wasn't that proof of high quality? After all, a rich and beautiful woman had been wearing that shirt, and a smashingly talented Western designer had created the *haute couture* garments for elegant ladies. I could see them in my mind's eye ambling along the Seine River to visit Notre Dame de Paris Cathedral. It was possible that even one of Germany's richest self-made ladies had possessed this particular item of clothing. On his daughter, the shirt looked like a dead man hanging on a gallows. The young hyena looked disgustingly shabby and I was convinced she deserved shabby treatment. That was how she went to school — in my Seine River outfit. I believed secondhand clothing was actually evidence of high status, wasn't it? In my opinion, it was weird that the insolent creature studied so hard.

She refused to pass the time of day with me, no "good morning", and no "good afternoon" if you know what I mean. Of course, why on earth should I cook or grill meat for her? What I gave her was rice, potatoes, and bread. She gorged herself on everything she could lay her paws on, no matter if it was fried chicken or turnips, shoving as much food into her mouth as it could hold. Since I didn't offer her anything to drink, she quaffed tap water like a horse. Honestly, I would have been disgusted if she'd used my drinking glasses. A lie has no legs, and the truth will out. Yes, she studied hard. It was the first time I'd seen a student read James Joyce. She read late into the night, and who paid the electricity bill? Me. She'd be cramming days on end in chemistry, physics, and math. She didn't even steal a glance at me as if I were a traffic light at an intersection she had no intention of crossing.

"Are you really in love with a girl?" I asked her. She didn't answer me. I held a piece of bread in my hand and a chunk of cheese. This was what I usually had for dinner — white cheese was a nutri-ent-dense food, and comparatively cheap. She looked up from the geometry problem she'd been hunching over all night, snatched the cheese from my hand, and gulped it down in one bite.

I put up with her for two months! I hoped Eustatius would call me. I hoped he'd write me a letter, drop me an email, text me, send me a photograph or a video… I prayed he'd get on the phone for a minute, for three seconds. On my birthday, March 13, he didn't call, and the reason became brutally clear to me. Eustatius had died. There was simply no other plausible explanation. He loved me. He couldn't breathe without me. He dedicated a poem to every square inch of my skin. He was dead. I knew it. That Wednesday I didn't have to teach classes and made up my mind to visit the public cemetery. The wind was stiff, and I was almost frozen to death as I looked for an abandoned grave. I found one — a rusty fence, the tombstone split down the middle, weeds and thorns all over the place, a downright scary picture.

I had honed the butcher knife I had inherited from my father, God bless his soul; Dad used it to cut the big bones when we slaughtered the hog. I fought a short but bloody war against the thorns and the weeds at the abandoned grave. I cut, cut, and cut until the grave sparkled, perfectly clean and wonderful. I borrowed five thousand levs from a distant cousin, and within a week I acquired a tombstone for Eustatius Cyril Eustatius. I knew neither the date of his birth nor his death date, but I tried to promote esthetical harmony in the cemetery park, so I inscribed **9 November 1973 — 12 November 2023** on Eustatius's tombstone. Then I was sure his grave looked like all other normal ones in the cemetery. I put Eustatius's photo on his tombstone as well, the only picture I'd taken of him with my camera — while he was eating my fish stew with great relish, enjoying every bite. He looked gorgeous in that picture, and I loved it. After Eustatius kissed me, I would hardly look at another man. No, sir, I wouldn't!

I paid two thousand levs to have his obituary published in the local newspapers, and I glued it on the wall of his apartment building to expose its contents to public view.

For another hundred levs, I had seven copies of my own death notice printed on wonderful glossy paper. I had included my best photograph in the notice; I was in the 1782-lev coat, the only one I had not bought from the second-hand store, and the only article of clothing Eustatius had taken with him. I hope he sold it at a profit before he met his maker, the gentle soul he was. Why did I publish my own obituary? I did it in order to make my intention clear to everyone, including myself: a lonely, stupid woman had died. She had been crushed by low self-esteem and fear of slipping into penury. This obituary note marked the birth of a lady whom Eustatius had loved — beautiful, witty, worthy of admiration and affection, her loyalty extolled and glorified. I was this lady! May the devil take this vile world! Rise up to meet magnificent Martha! Martha would be the winner. Eustatius, you can see me from heaven. You protect me from heaven, I can feel it! I love you!

The first step I took after I glued Eustatius's death notice on the wall of his apartment building was to collect his daughter's textbooks — not second-hand, of course, 192nd-hand they all were! I crammed them into a black garbage bag, and I shoved her clothes — each piece of which cost less than fifty cents — into a second garbage bag. Of course, I didn't throw out two of my denim shirts the young vandal had worn without my express permission. I intended to wash them with lice-killer laundry detergent. I had a fundamental weakness — I got emotionally attached to my clothes.

I waited for the young hooligan to get home from school — to my amazement she didn't drink, didn't even smoke. Well, where could she get the money for such pleasures, in the first place? She didn't do drugs eithers, and was constantly boning up for various tests and exams. Why did freaks like her keep their noses to the grindstone, while normal young people didn't? I threw the two garbage bags out on the bottom of the staircase. I flatly refused to let her come inside my room and spread the vile second-hand store smell in the apartment building.

"You won't set foot in my place again," I informed her as I stood behind my locked front door. "Your father is dead."

The she-ass — as sometimes I impolitely addressed her — neither bellowed as I expected, though I'd really welcome her howls of anguish, nor did she spit on the clean floor outside my door as I had feared. She uttered some words that robbed me of my mental equilibrium for weeks, "You're a record holder, with the longest period of time you've housed me in your flat. Forty-seven days altogether. His other girlfriends toughed it out a fortnight at most."

Who? The other girlfriends? Other women? My dearest Eustatius!

Of course the she-ass was lying. A nasty bimbo. A worm! A bucket of smelly slime — that was what she was! The insufferable bullies among my high school students were fragile rosebuds compared to her. A weasel! An unbearable, scheming hustler!

I didn't know any breathing technique to help me calm down, so I bought the most expensive candles on the market — I'd go hungry for days on account of that — and I lit ten of these at a time on Eustatius's grave. I kept his last resting place in perfect condition — with lovely flowers, as tidy as my dear parents' tomb. The sight of it brought peace to my tortured soul. Eustatius, my love, you made a woman out of me. The rag who was lonely and ugly, poker-faced and dull, breathed her last. I myself wrote her obituary. Now I am a beautiful, clever and generous creature. A lady. I love you, Eustatius!

—⁂—

"A can of cheap ale!" he said to himself every time he thought he was about to grow sad or restless. Melancholy? Sorrow? Come off it! Life is stale beer, and I am healthy. I can drink as much as I want, so, dull existence, be prepared. I will devour you and I make no bones about it. Either way, you have an end, miserable life. One day, I'll cash in my chips too; therefore, life, you're no bigger than me, no reason to feel contempt for my instructions. I am your superior. I'll show you who's who.

He went out for long walks along the most upscale streets in Sofia, the capital of the country. He'd target his efforts on creatures in elegant dresses, but it was not good looks alone that attracted him. What was the meaning of good looks these days? A load of cosmetics plus "in-depth discussions" with psychologists, that gang of rapacious muggers who suggested to the young bird she was charming, independent, smart, etc., and soon the bird's self-confidence bordered on breathtaking arrogance.

One cared about her looks for five weeks, and not a day more. "A pretty face is an open door to financial resources," he thought. Finance is not a load of cosmetics. A belle was either born rich, or has married a big fat wallet. Ladies of this type were as easily visible as the moon in the evening sky. The glamour, the sense of opulence, the whims and extravagant gestures were the alphabet those duchesses used to describe their lives with. Wealth was *embedded* in generations of big wheels raised amidst lavish productions of Mozart, pomposity, and oceans of highfalutin' words, expensive vacations at fashionable ski resorts around the world. One couldn't go wrong with a woman like that. The most urgent priority was to charm her *brilliant* mind. The belle had the arrogance to believe she was the sole heiress of splendor. He had to subdue her despite her self-reliance and clothes created by glamorous fashion designers. In the long run, he captured her eyes, at once insolent and expectant. Herr von Eustatius had no intention of doing anything heroic other than reciting and, at a later stage, dedicating a poem or two. Those were the motives behind his leisurely strolls along the streets.

He'd been spending all his savings on his good looks, Giorgio Armani jackets, Hugo Boss blazers, and sport coats — he could endure weeks of starvation, but he'd get an Armani suit and would bask in the designer's reputation for impeccable tailoring. He looked like a young god. He did. He, Eustatius, was the power that ordered the cosmos of love which way to go, forward or backward. He was not the sun, he was the force by which a planet drew objects toward its center; he was gravity that nudged the sun to follow its boring orbit in the universe. And what was a universe — an opportunity for cunning astronomers to make money and bear grand scientific titles? Eustatius, however, didn't care about astronomy. He was interested in ambitious women and the level of prestige and privilege they'd attained. He could live happily with one of these ever after. It is true everyone has their own ideas of happiness. He'd opt for healthy food, a comfortable house, sparklingly clean and warm, and, preferably, cooks and kitchen maids who were interested in scrupulous hygiene. He didn't want his woman to smell of floor disinfectants and greasy meals. Would a female individual be his kindred spirit if she polished the toilets? She would be a servant, but Eustatius wanted a lady by his side.

So he found Fernanda; no one called her Fernanda, of course. Her name at birth was Fanka. Her father, once a porter, a dirt-poor bugger, had become a large-scale dealer, first in vegetables and scrap metal, then in chemicals, whatever that meant. If, by accident, folks happened to rub shoulders with her father and made him angry in the process of communication, they'd soon end up under a cheap tombstone or were transferred with surprising expediency to the city morgue. However, a guy's end was another guy's beginning, wasn't it?

Fernanda's mother still bought her knitting yarn from the Frog market. Unable to break a number of habits she'd had for years as a porter's wife, she counted her pennies and froze her gardener's wages years on end. The old woman no longer cooked anything; she hired a maid, and called her, in keeping with modern trends, "domestic help" or "skilled kitchen staff." The skilled staff, the poor maid, ran fourteen hours a day around the house, sweeping the floors, disinfecting, polishing crystal glasses, and was obliged to address Fernanda's mother as "Madam."

Eustatius chose the name Fernanda for Fanka. She was a girl who had trouble studying, but she held two degrees in Ecology (Ph.D.) and in Ancient History from two prestigious liberal arts colleges in Bulgaria. She had gone and tried to complete four semesters of study in literary translation in the USA, and had lived in London for no less than two and a half years to learn English. The girl had her limitations achieving this goal, a fact that did not prevent Fanka-Fernanda and her parents from claiming that the "princess" spoke *perfectly* Shakespeare's language. They all were very proud they had heard the name Shakespeare. The fact that they could pronounce it made a huge difference, even though the porter and his wife did not know who the guy was and what he did for a living.

Eustatius won Fanka's heart with his Gucci shoes. He took her like a fortress whose defenders had single-handedly broken the latch of the steel gate, and with considerable impatience had laid a soft, red carpet at his feet. The first night. Eustatius refused to follow Fernanda to her luxurious home in Sofia, Bulgaria. He kissed her hand and quoted Alfred de Musset's famous thought, "*The most disagreeable that your worst enemy says to your face does not approach what your best friends say behind your back.*" The girl, of course, did not know who this Alfred was; on the other hand, she was ready to explore this line of thinking further, or at least she said so. Eustatius had tried out more famous authors like Faulkner and Turgenev on Fernanda — his own untidy daughter read Turgenev — but Fanka, alas, had heard their names quite seldom. Lord, Eustatius could hardly put up with her for a long period of time.

Her house was beautiful. It was built by people who understood how to decorate a palatial residence and had been paid a lot. The rooms were furnished by arbiters of architectural taste and designers who had seen the *Swan Lake Dance of the Cygnets* at least twice in their lives. Flowers from the four continents of the world bloomed in the endless courtyard. An important detail: three cooks worked for Fernanda, which suited Eustatius fine. Everything that surrounded him was clean, polished, and glittering in harmony with the smiles of a very pretty housekeeper. On the other hand, the poet had learned by experience how damaging it was to ogle the maid in the presence of her mistress. He'd toss the phrase 'the lackadaisical one', making it clear he meant exactly the damsel, and Fanka was happy. She provided Eustatius with a spacious room, a masseur, a psychologist, a professor of modern American literature with whom Eustatius drank wine twice a week and kept up an intellectual conversation.

Fanka could not sail across any intellectual sea no matter how shallow its waters, but she ate eco, bio and organic foods. Two fitness instructors holding a Cambridge medical degree each took care of her physical condition; psychologists from Furtwangen University — where the hell was that, Germany, Austria? — were in charge of her excellent mental health; a prominent comedian was hired to cheer her up with witty jokes and epigrams when the need arose. A diploma *humanist*, whatever that meant, recited love poetry to her.

After Eustatius took Fanka's dreams by storm, the heiress dispensed with the services provided by the humanist and the two psychologists. She declared to her parents that she had never been happier in her entire life. Fanka's father, Doko, the porter, and Stoya his wife who, out of habit, still crocheted using cheap yarn she procured from the Frog Market, wholeheartedly approved of Eustatius — he was not one of those brownnosers who waited, their tongues lolling, ready to lick the toilet bowl clean. Eustatius could converse in Bulgarian, but he spoke English, French, and German as well as other languages that didn't exist, but Doko and his wife didn't suspect any foul play.

Eustatius drank moderately and avoided gorging himself on caviar, truffles or other expensive foods, so he passed the test Stoya had put him to — he got his fill of her homemade specialty, roasted peppers with garlic. Besides, the future son-in-law could use a knife to cut his pork chop with, didn't spit on the floor after a glass or two, didn't even swear; yet at a certain point, he took to effing and blinding the local government, which made Stoya believe he was a great man.

A month after he moved in with Fanka, the young woman changed her name to Fernanda through the appropriate steps provided by law. Very rarely in the evening, after nice healthy sex, Eustatius felt sad. It was not a distinct feeling, it was a weight in the pit of his stomach at the thought of his daughter. He couldn't stop thinking about her. It made him weak, drained his ability to quote beautiful sentences formulated by great people who weren't great at all, hell, they'd just been lucky enough to have someone else pay their bills and record their ramblings while they were drunk: some fat Fernanda did it for them.

The great thinkers had usually grown up in golden cradles and, champing on the bit, the whole dynasty of relatives awaited the offspring's birth, so that the millions would fall into the hands of the lawful heir. The literary titans had described what any poor bugger could cobble together if he didn't have to toil and moil sixteen hours a day for his bread; if his wife, having the brains of a starving hyena, had not been babbling on about his incompetence; if the baby had not been howling in her crib, sucking at the last drop of her father's energy, draining the funds from his wallet and bank account.

Eustatius was angry with tiny Anna, his daughter, who damn it, was dear to him, so dear that in order to live like a normal person, he had to get rid of her. Eustatius had to throw her out of his mind the way he dumped his shirt torn at the elbows. He sat still over her crib instead. His thoughts went back to the kid's black eyes, and didn't go away. This happened often — when he wasn't particularly good at his writing job, when the editors had rejected his new manuscript, when he was sick and tired of his wife, a Bulgarian literature teacher who day in, day out, cooked tinned soup for him; or when Eustatius was about to smash the skull of the nitwit who hit his car at the round-about. He liked the child and said to himself, "A devil of a time!" Of course there are no devils. Guys made them up to justify their own greed and envy. He remembered the day when he wished the girl with the black eyes would die. Her hair was as thick as nettles, damn it. If the little worm kicked the bucket, Eustatius would be free. He wouldn't give any thought to his wife's soups.

His daughter had grown up. He couldn't explain why he would dash into the dingy one-room flat where she lived, her smoldering dark eyes hating him. Climbing the stairs to her place was stupid of Eustatius. The kid refused to talk to him. She was made of the same pig iron, well, not iron, the same biting frost as her mother. The girl kept mum, turned down the money he offered her, and pointed to the front door. Then Eustatius, the bloody fool, still remembered that summer he took his daughter to the seaside, not with Fanka. It had been another Fernanda.

Eustatius couldn't stand women who didn't know who Flannery O'Connor or Françoise Sagan was. Those dim-witted butterflies of the fair sex cooked magnificent evening meals for him, made passionate love, but he quickly quenched his thirst, and the meals got tiresome. He and a Fernanda took his daughter to Sozopol, the famous Bulgarian Black Sea resort. On the third day Eustatius sent his girlfriend packing, and remained with his daughter. The two of them rode the Ferris wheel, and swam together. He bought new

clothes for little Anna on Fernanda's money. A stupid thing he did —
collected his child's old rags in a bag from Lidl store, the big German
grocery chain, and dumped them in a dumpster.

She cried buckets. No words slipped out of her mouth. Anna
hadn't been a garrulous kid since birth. There were days when Eustatius doubted whether his daughter was normal at all; he was convinced she was not. He said to himself that it would've been better if
the little caterpillar had breathed her last, there and then. No more
foolish doubts would crucify him. How could this child be normal?
So much affection had been wasted between Eustatius and his wife,
so much impossible heat. Nature tolerated no excesses. Eustatius
believed that if there was too much love, idiots were born, and made
an appointment for Anna to see a psychiatrist, a famous professor.

"I'm afraid she is weird… deranged," Eustatius spoke bluntly,
looking the professor in the eye. "Persons who live with a mental
disorder should understand what a gigantic mistake their birth was."

The professor stared and kept silent as he examined the girl. He
took a blood sample, and after a week told Eustatius, "Your daughter
is a perfectly healthy child." The examination cost an arm and a leg.
Eustatius paid for it with Fernanda's money. The professor insisted
on a dozen more blood tests. Eustatius paid for everything. The tests
confirmed that Anna was perfectly healthy, but he continued to have
his doubts. He still had them. His daughter's dark eyes watched him
intently, a gaze of frozen gravel that put a wall up in front of him.

The thought of Anna filled him with sadness. Eustatius wanted
to suppress it, drive it away, so he visited his daughter's school, and
talked to her class teacher. He asked the pedagogue, quite casually by
the way, what problems his only child posed for her classmates. To

his astonishment, the teacher — big as a hill, in her early forties — said that Anna was the best student in her class, a Valedictorian! She didn't have any poor grades, her essays on contemporary Bulgarian and English literature were brilliant, and she won a gold medal at the international math competition in India last September! Her paper on the topic "Dignity" won the first prize provided by some private foundation, a famous one, whose name, alas, escaped the teacher.

"Does she have friends?" asked Eustatius. The instructor's face darkened. Eustatius could read words written on rusting human faces.

"She is an excellent student, and they are not," replied Ms. Big Hill. "Anna does not talk to them. She doesn't talk to me, either. What she wrote in her essay speaks for her. She makes them feel like they are — what should I say — they are no geniuses, which, to be honest, they are not," the oval lady sighed.

Eustatius knew love was not a log fire crackling in a fireplace. It was the ruined forest after the blaze, black charred trunks, wisps of ash floating up, no pine needles. Anna, his daughter, wrote essays. Eustatius had written essays, too. They had won literary prizes, his essays. His books seemed to offer hope to admirers of contemporary Bulgarian literature. Eustatius gave private lessons in creative writing to well-to-do young men and women, pampered youths and their girlfriends who'd grown up in platinum diapers. Belligerent literary clans worshipped Eustatius because he instilled confidence into the scions of the well-established Bulgarian families that the young talents would one day soon make the world admire their work. Their work my foot! Eustatius told the parents their wonderful children would be professors, researchers, shrewd businessmen, industrialists, and entrepreneurs of tomorrow. Their discoveries would astound old and tired Europe, Eustatius was firmly convinced a bright future awaited them. No doubt about it! Yes, if pigs could fly, his ex-wife used to say.

It must have been his mom's fault that Eustatius remained a worthless nerd.

"Don`t cheat, son. If you don't hurt anybody, you won't live in vain," his mother told him once. That was a downright lie. If you didn't hurt the other guy, he'd rip your head off with the teeth that you didn't knock out. He'd pick your pocket and steal your bottom dollar with the right hand you didn't break. He'd get you thrown out of work and take your place at the big wheel's table. He'd blow the gaff on your opinion about your publisher's asinine submission policy, and your new novel would be rejected for publication. Eustatius's mother brought him up to believe in honesty. That was the wrong thing to do.

Eustatius didn't attend her funeral. She had roasted him over the open fire of her naivety.

"You should know, Eti — that was what she called him. — Eti. It's been a long time since the monkeys became men, son. Perhaps more than a million years ago. That long time stays in every man's blood and in every woman's. It means that men and women — because they are human — can feel if they've done ugly things to others. Even if a guy owns a mountain of money, and chauffeurs drive him to posh restaurants, and put a red carpet under his feet, the guy can't forget. The time during which the monkey's been toiling and moiling to become a man, those millions of years, speak to us. They tell each one of us we've done an evil thing to somebody else. The time won't let us forget. All the money, cars and women you have (why did you break up with your wife, Eti? She was so pretty, that woman of yours), all the dough and credit cards in your wallet won't help. The million years know you are no good. And they repeat it to you. You know you're worse than slime. It eats your liver from the inside like that disease, the worst one."

That was why Eustatius didn't attend his mother's funeral. Often, he could not sleep at night. The years in which the monkey toiled to become a man tortured him. He watched the funeral from the nearby hill. His mother's coffin shook in a battered pickup truck. The truck stopped, and his daughter and a fat guy got out of it. The fatso stared at his phone. Did he watch a porn video all the time the funeral lasted? The priest was drunk. It was clear he spluttered only a tenth of what he'd been paid for. Anna, his daughter, didn't notice a thing. She didn't say anything to the priest or to the fat guy with the phone. She cried, her hands clutching her grandmother's coffin. Eustatius thought it was a bad idea he'd come. Why had he seen all this? He shouldn't have.

Sometimes, after good, healthy sex with Fernanda, Eustatius was filled with sadness. Sadness is the sister of death, his mom had said. Life's a cheap drink. The important thing is to be thirsty and guzzle life every day, lots of it. Even though Eustatius ran six miles a day, he did not get tired enough to escape from the thoughts of his wife. Anna. That was the name he had given his daughter, his wife's name, the woman who had made him forget he could breathe. It lasted for months, longer than a year. At that time, Eustatius did not think about money. His Armani jackets meant nothing to him, his short stories seemed to write themselves. He didn't admire his private students who gave him a feeling of financial well-being and got on his nerves. Anna. Wasting so much love was immoral, an impossibility. No one in his right mind could outlive or outlast it. He saw Anna everywhere, on the fading TV screen, in his palms, in the shadow of the poplar trees beside the road, near the dumpsters, in the resplendent homes of his private students. He ran like mad to her.

"You're a poor writer," she told him. "A good writer doesn't copy from people's lives. He doesn't make love to Anna to describe lovemaking in his pathetic books. A great writer creates a world for Anna. If the world he has dumped her in is a false one, Anna goes away."

"You think I make too little money and I'm not rich enough for you?" he asked her.

"You don't write well enough," she said. On the following day her clothes were gone, his designer suits the parents of his ingenious private students had given him were gone, and even their daughter's toys were gone. Eustatius ran to the Frog Market and saw all: a stranger was wearing his Armani jacket. His clothes, her expensive blouses, and their daughter's toys lay on old newspapers on the ground, and each piece cost one lev. Eustatius bought up all the items, his wife's clothes, the little one's toys, and his suits.

He paid.

"Where did the woman go after she sold these rags to you?" he asked the large Roma woman, the stall keeper. She was a bombshell all right.

"The lady said her hubby was stingy. 'He's good for nothing,' the lady said to me," replied the Roma gal beautiful as the sky, so Eustatius made her pack up the stall at once. He took this pretty femme to his flat, and asked her to sit down by the crib in which his daughter was whimpering. Eustatius paid the baby no heed. He kissed his pretty guest instead. The Roma chick was barefoot and had no clothes under her crumpled Armani dress.

Eustatius's daughter started wailing. The gypsy's love was good. It put his skin on fire, but he couldn't drive Anna's skin out of his mind.

He saw his wife although she was not there.

He saw Anna.

"I've had enough of you," he told the Roma woman.

The gypsy didn't call down curses on him.

"You are in a pickle," she said. "You can't hear the brat because of an old skirt. You're cooked."

Eustatius could still hear little Anna sobbing. He'd chosen the tot's name himself to be sure that her mom's blood ran in her name — Anna. Strong blood. Rich and vindictive. His friends (he had no friends for sure) said, "You're much more attractive than your ex-wife, Eustatius. She was a bad bargain through and through. How could you be so foolish to marry her?"

Little Anna had bawled and choked on her own tears. Eustatius burned her mother's clothes and watched as they caught fire one by one on the bathroom floor. Then, for the first and last time in his life, Eustatius wept. No one saw him. Half an hour later he was smiling, as the child sobbed and said there were snakes in her tummy.

If his wife hadn't gone, if she hadn't sold his suits, her skirts, and the little one's toys, maybe Eustatius would've had a home, too. Maybe he would have obtained a university chair. He would come back home in the evenings like all normal people. Anna might have cooked chicken stew for dinner, or he could heat up a creamy soup.

Little Anna would ask him, "Daddy what is the past tense form of the verb 'to weave'?"

Eustatius would grumble, "Look it up in the dictionary," but he'd be proud of her. Such a kid, young and thin, asking him about an irregular verb. Little Anna had told him she wanted to weave a cage for a grasshopper.

In English, "to weave" means "to intertwine".

"Don't weave a cage for a grasshopper," Eustatius had explained to her. "Grasshoppers die if you put them in a cage."

"She doesn't talk to anyone," his daughter's teacher had told Eustatius. "She keeps herself to herself, sits alone, doesn't speak much, reads... But her essays.... actually, I already told you. Anna has received the national competition essay award twice, and…"

Eustatius cut off the teacher mid-sentence. He didn't say "Thank you, Ma'am" or "Goodbye" to her. He turned his back on the peda-gogue and left her office.

Eustatius could not stand it any longer.

After half an hour, everything lined up brilliantly. He smiled broadly as he returned to his temporary home. Fernanda greeted him with an ardent kiss.

I WAS WAITING FOR Nikolai in his room. I'd slipped in through the barely noticeable hole which I'd been cutting in the hedge - for two long weeks. I had donned my shabby faux-fur coat and I was cold. Rosen had promised to hoist me onto the terrace, but didn't turn up, so I began to suspect that I'd be cooked. My classmates believed that to cook someone's goose meant to dump the damsel somewhere with a sack wrapped around her head, so all the waifs and strays could have a bite of her lard. In my chemistry class, they didn't wrap a sack around me. They tied my face with my own blue coat, an article of clothing they'd soaked in urine. The garment cost a buck at the second-hand store.

I felt trouble was brewing when in the whole math class there were two Bs, the rest were just Cs — apparently, the students had copied from the only person who'd solved two of the problems. Those problems were so dumb and transparent that they seemed to have been stitched together with rags. I got an A⁺ on the test and refused to let anyone copy from my notebook. It was clear to me I was far from radiantly perfect in mathematics, but I didn't leave a stone unturned and a problem unsolved in my math textbooks.

Mrs. Lacheva, our math teacher, as thin as a firefly, once said to me, "I have a new problem book for you...why do you put your shoulder to the wheel all the time?" Then she whispered, as if someone had pressed an axe against her throat, "I'm afraid for you, Anna. I didn't tell them you were the only one with an A⁺. Someone's taken a peek at my teacher's notebook. I can give you a C and you'll be like them all if you want. What would you say to that?"

"No, Ms. Lacheva," I said. "I got my excellent grade and I did not cheat."

This Lacheva woman had absent-minded, light brown eyes — like the soil Grandma dug to plant garlic in early spring. Very patiently, Grandma taught me how to do it. At a certain point, she told me, "Anna, remember, if you want your strawberries not to droop and wilt, plant garlic near the strawberry patch, girl."

I could plant no garlic because my father sold the field to some big shot from Sofia, the capital of the country, and I was left hanging, with no strawberries or onions in sight. My father wanted to sell Grandma's home as well, but a long time ago, just before Grandpa died — as she lay in bed with a glass of water in hand — Grandma bequeathed her one-room flat to me. I didn't know what exactly that meant, but after my father couldn't sell the thing, I found out that if a home was bequeathed to you, you could live in your grandmother's room, sleep in her bed, and pray for her to come and stay with you in your dreams.

The old one did come and stay. This happened during the week when I told Ms. Lacheva, my quiet and magnificent math teacher, "I solved all the problems. I didn't copy from anyone. I do deserve an A.$^{+}$"

She said, "Okay," and walked away, her footsteps whispering, as if it were raindrops, not shoes,   this woman wore. It was because of her that I loved the rain.

"'You have a talent for math," she'd told me. "You have a brilliant mind." She didn't know this was wrong. The mind grows when a girl is lonely. What else could grow under her skin but the mind? The poor thing is imprisoned in the skull and can't go anywhere. What else can it do, but grow inside the girl, illuminating her bones and blood?

I was waiting for Nikolai. Rosen had beat it and left me in the lurch. From now on, there would be no one to lift me onto Nikolai's terrace.

"Do you want me to teach you to kiss?" Rosen had asked me. I didn't want to and he went off the deep end. His big hand pushed me and I fell hard on my back.

"You're off your rocker," he hissed. "I stopped barking because you said it was stupid of me, you see."

What should I do? I got up from the dry patch of land where his blow had sent me sprawling. It used to be a garden for a time, but now it was dried mud with the tire tracks of old Opel cars.

"I'm sorry, man. I want you to teach me how to kiss, but I have a rotten tooth. My mouth is full of bacteria."

Rosen hardly knew what "bacteria" was.

"A girl's been talking to me. She's waited for you for hours, Anna. Said she wanted to marry you," Rosen spoke rapidly. "So do I. My mom says you're not all there. That's the reason you have bacteria. It's because of that... girl."

I came up closer to him, but he pushed me hard again. This time I didn't fall. I'd learned to get up no matter how badly they kicked me.

"Will you lift me onto Nikolai's terrace tonight?" I asked. Rosen kissed me. He'd eaten garlic, or maybe there was garlic in the sausage the kitchen maid had made his sandwich with. The woman cooked, and cleaned the house Rosen's mother was so proud of.

"I'll lift you onto that terrace, all right," he said. "Come back at 6 pm sharp."

It was 7.30 pm. I knew I was cooked. Rosen had given me the slip.

Then I remembered. The coat had been soaked in urine. They'd tied it tightly around my head with a pair of pantyhose. I found out afterwards that the pantyhose was quite expensive. I'm not a sentimental person. Two days after I recovered from the thrashing, I wiggled into it and went to school.

I got a few kicks. My classmates hit and bit me. I hate to describe where someone kissed me, or should I say "chomped me"? They didn't speak. They acted fast, pinched and clawed at my boobs. My skin hurt worst around the belly button. I found out the hard way how one paid if one got an A$^+$ in math. For almost a month, I gadded about town blue in the face, my belly button purple and ugly; however, on the very next day after my urine-soaked coat was wrapped around my mouth, I solved one of the hardest SAT math problems on the blackboard in front of the math class. Lacheva said, "I'm convinced you have a talent for math, Anna."

My grandmother had mentioned that Mom was excellent in math. I didn't know exactly what my mother did for a living, she used to live in three different states. Once she gave me three hundred euros and filled my fridge with pork chops and sausages.

"Your father is a master criminal," she said. "He left you in that shithole. I send him money to pay for your upkeep."

I liked my grandmother's one-room flat. I used to go out late in the evenings, so no one noticed me at the Frog Market. I collected the empty plastic crates thrown in the dustbins, took them to the expensive market next to the imposing City Bank building, and sold them for 50 cents apiece. I dragged bundles of waste paper and sold them to the recycling center. I collected beer bottles and cans; that was why I loved the drunkards, those wonderful ships sailing in the sea of alcohol. Every time I saw a bombed carouser, I felt pity for him, because I knew the hogwash, fake stuff through and through, they sold at *The King and the General*, the scrappiest pub near the Frog Market. Grandpa used to buy his brandy there, and that was why he dropped dead. He closed the earth behind him, and the two of us, Grandma and I, remained all alone in the world, two hungry pigeons in the middle of winter. I lugged the stoned guy to his place. They were heavy as mountains, those drinking men.

"Come on, buddy," I said to the carouser. "Move that leg of yours forward. Now move the other one. That's a good boy!"

In the beginning, the wives were jealous, but if I went to collect drunkards, I put on clothes that had been thrown away in black sacks even by the second-hand store, so the tipplers' wives buried the hatchet.

"Anna, put this in your pocket," the faithful wife would say by way of thank you. The femmes gave me fifty pennies, one lev, two levs at the most. However, there were a few generous souls among them who usually gave me something to eat. I sold Grandma's fridge a long time ago — God bless her soul — so I guzzled all the bread and sausages I was given on the way back home before the food could go bad.

It wasn't a bad place at all, my little room: Grandma's bed was so warm! I often put on Grandma's old coat, and kept Grandpa's parka, although I could have grabbed a lot of money for these items from the peddlers at the Frog Market. Grandma's and Grandpa's clothes kept me much warmer than the jackets I bought for a fiver once every six months at the Second-chance store at the intersection of Levski Street and Summer Avenue. It was the most gorgeous shop in town probably because Levski, the Bulgarian national hero, liked me for no reason at all and helped me from heaven to focus my attention on the best merchandise available.

That bodyguard, Rosen, why did he stab me in the back? How could I climb up to Nikolai's terrace by myself? A cherry tree jutted out near the open window, not a normal tree, a messy cloud of blossoms it was, and the branches didn't seem reliable at all as I looked at them. Carefully, like a mosquito, I clung to the tree trunk. Then even more carefully — it felt like I were a tapeworm for I knew from my biology textbook that tape worms had suckers — I clutched at the branch that looked as thin as a dying man's breath. Inch by inch, I crawled along it towards the terrace. At the same time, I was cautiously planning not to fall on my head. If I did, I could hurriedly join Grandma among the clouds far from pain, rage, or rancor.

"Do you know why I bit you *there*?" asked Julian, one of my classmates, who at one time sold marijuana, but he agreed to suspend activity after his father bought him a Mercedes. "You should know that I wanted to do something else," he continued. "And I would've done it. But that idiot, the slut in love with you, she beat me to it."

"'If you touch me one more time, I will kill you," I told him. He, the wastefully tall and burly Julian, backed away. To me, the ugliest name in the world is Julian.

"What about her? Will you let her?" grinned clubby Julian, but didn't dare to kick me.

I hung from the branch like a caterpillar dangling by the slimy thread of its own excretory system; however, I had no thread. I'd probably have no excretory system to speak of if I plummeted to the tiles. I dangled from the cherry tree, clutching the branch. Soon I'd founder on the granite alley below me. Hopefully I wouldn't break my ribs. Broken legs, I'd heard, healed fast. One, two, three. Breathe!! One, two, three!

I did a back-and-forth, then again a back-and-forth swing and in a last-ditch effort, like a wasp whose head had been cut off but its wings keep fluttering, after a wild thrust I thumped loudly onto the terrace. I wobbled, shook and bent my knees. Good. Nothing was broken. Like a lizard, I climbed onto the pot with that wretched flower and squeezed through the open bathroom window. "God," as my father once said. "You don't exist. People made you up so they'd have someone to worship. If a guy doesn't pray to some bogus deity, he could as well send a bullet into his brain." My God, what if the bathroom window had been closed... Through the bathroom, quietly and deftly as a breeze, I slipped into Nikolai's room.

Rosen, the son of pancake Zoe, the insignificant department head at one of the ministries in Sofia, wrote me a letter once. This curious epistle read, "He can't do the job."

I had never seen a more attractive man than Nikolai. Black hair, pale face, blue-green eyes, intelligent gaze.

Nikolai lay in bed, focused on his phone. I dropped the shabby faux-fur coat at his feet and faced him — my black T-shirt was crumpled, my black shorts looked like a bun gone bad; scars and bruises were all over my legs, bloody furrows appeared purple from wrists to elbows on my forearms. The bark of that vile cherry tree was thick, and the small branches, like a handful of nails, had gouged holes in my skin.

I stood in front of the most handsome guy, blood dripping from my fingers onto the floor — onto the gorgeous, light wood which shimmered like the Dead Sea and as warm as its waters. Nikolai took a brief glimpse at me and focused on his phone again. I thought to myself, "You're quite stupid, Anna. The bruises from the nasty pinching and biting haven't gone away yet. He'll think you're sick."

"You might think I'm sick," I said.

He studied his phone as he gave me a cursory glance, then stared at the glossy screen again. I felt like I was a vast empty space. Damn it! The devil take the hindmost — even though according to the

Theory of Relativity there are no devils — I had to act. As my father used to say, 'Better get a drubbing, than stand like a monument that has nothing else to do, but jut out and make people ashamed they haven't knocked it down yet." Nikolai, that magnificent apparition, scrutinized his phone as I towered above a wooden statue of a lovely naked Dead Sea youth. I could have given the nude piece of art to some artist who sold his paintings a dime a dozen at the Frog market; most watercolorist starved before they sold a still life. I had a feeling that the artists, poor buggers all, were worse off than me.

What was I whining and sobbing for! I had successfully crawled up that abominable Canadian or maybe Ethiopian cherry tree, I had squeezed through the bathroom window left slightly ajar and I had dangled from a damned bough seven feet above the terrace. I pulled it off with such ease as if I'd only stepped on a broken paving slab. I stood near the most handsome boy; his mother, wealthy beyond my notions of propriety, had pulled a few strings to get the headmaster's blessing, so her magnificent son read poetry to us, the lowborn. Most Bulgarian literary magazines published articles proclaiming Nikolai Caramelitev was a genius. A genius my foot! A magazine would declare a worm was a genius as long as a financial heavyweight had paid enough. Anyone could name a pile of rubble "poetry" if you bought him a glass of brandy at Lilliput Café.

The most wonderful boy kept gaping at his phone as blood kept on oozing from my open wounds. What should I do? Run back through the bathroom, creep down the bough of the cherry tree, jump — and land on my face? No. "If they beat you, hold your head high," my father had said. Only he and Grandma told me a thing or two. At times, I read about a few great ideas in my textbooks, but somebody had been paid to write them, and when somebody took money for something, it was not wisdom. It was a commodity.

I headed for the door with my head raised like the national flag. The door was made of beautiful wood. The Dead Sea had died for no other reason: they had stolen its wood from which some very skilled carpenter had carved this sturdy door, a smiling wooden sun, ogling the statue of the naked youth, his nose turned up at me. I'm a girl, and they don't want me here, I thought as I walked with my head held proudly high as a national flag.

"Rosen has reported to me that you are going to get on my nerves tonight," said the poet who did not write poetry. He piled nonsense onto paper instead.

—⁓—

I proceeded to the door as calmly as if I were at the Frog Market looking for a pair of sneakers. The most magnificent boy in the world got up slowly from his mattress. No matter how high I lifted my head, it was impossible not to notice something I had long been dreaming of noticing. Not his shoulders, of course, which sagged like an empty pillowcase; not his skin that was pale and hairless like a girl's. Not his thin, long fingers. I trudged forward doggedly like the old women who clutched boxes stuffed with freshly plucked nettles for sale at the Frog Market.

Nikolai was a step away from my back. My T-shirt was torn because that nasty cherry tree had caught it. My trousers were soaked with blood mixed with dust, and felt like a scab. Without haste or agitation, Nikolai removed my torn T-shirt. He put something on my shoulders, maybe a towel, but it was too light and flimsy.

Could be a silk shawl, a fine one; then the bard pushed me toward the carved door in whose afternoon sunshine the statue of the naked youth was basking.

March on even if they hammered a nail into your skull. March on! I'd never kissed anyone or anything aside from Rosen's garlic-scented tongue, and that classmate of ours who made a failed attempt at a kiss after he untied the pee-stained coat from my head. I kissed Nikolai. He was very weak, the poor poet. I used to get the children ready for kindergarten when one of my neighbors was sick. The woman would give me a fiver and a cheap sandwich by way of thank you. The children I took care of were all beautiful. So far, no tot I was responsible for had ever fallen down, tripped, or lost their water bottle.

The kids' fingers I had washed so many times before kindergarten were as thin and frail as Nikolai's ribs under my hands. I nudged him gently toward his phone, which was glowing on the pillow. The pillowcase was embroidered with the captivating figure of youth from the statue. Poor Nikolai! He had to sleep on the same cushion night after night. The poet refused to take a step towards the mattress with his phone gleaming on it. I nudged him again. He didn't move. This was what I had been used to — when the child screamed he hated his kindergarten and said No! No! to his teacher, I gently pushed the little one forward. The same thing happened with Nikolai: I did push him, very gently. He tried to fall to the floor, but I held him, of course.

If what happened had been love, I was the World War I howitzer placed outside the Town Hall to instill patriotism in me and my young classmates. Nikolai offered no resistance as he slumped to the floor. I suspected that golden threads were indeed woven into the lovely yellow wood. At some point, I discovered that the whole floor was an image of the same attractive youth of the statue who was innocently undressing. The artist had done his best to preserve the constantly changing play of shades and nuances enveloping the parts of the young body. Did it not occur to the maestro that, at best, the youth would experience muscle soreness?

Nikolai was more fragile than the kids I took to kindergarten in the morning. He lay still, his delicate ribs pressing his skin as translucent as apple juice. His hands, a pair of white slow fish, rested on the edge of the painting portraying the attractive youth. Nikolai's black hair waited, cradled in the painted swain's lap.

What now? Should I give up?

I didn't give up after all. Better try and fail than go away with your tail tucked between your legs. I had exactly the same situation every time I had to deal with the difficult math problems Ms. Lacheva selected for me. I failed at my first attempt. On the second try, I fell flat too. Thus, I came to know what the essence of love was — evident failure. In my opinion, I succeeded in the end, after a fashion. Nikolai lay, delicate, as thin as a trout, cool as butter kept in the fridge. O, my God, folks had invented you so they'd have someone to complain to, or blame for their own downfall! My God, why did I sell Grandma's fridge! If I hadn't, probably I would have known what to do with frozen butter. I couldn't determine if love had happened or not. That was the most substantial dimension of its essence — a girl didn't know if love existed or not. She could embrace whichever hypothesis she chose.

I had no time for hypotheses or wishful thinking. Nikolai stood up abruptly from the floor, his eyes a pair of switchblades. You push a button and the blade snaps out eager to kill.

With unexpected force, the poet gripped my shoulders and gave me a hefty shove. I fell over the statue of the poor young man who must have been shivering with cold. I was quite fortunate that my head didn't crash against the sun door. The poet used the soft shawl he had thrown over my shoulders to wipe his legs, then plunged his green gaze back into his phone. I stood like the Eiffel Tower, a totally miserable Eiffel Tower, and after a couple of seconds I bent down to get my T-shirt and pants, black and stained with my own blood. Nikolai showed no interest in my untidy clothes. If they don't give a tinker's damn about how you feel, hold your head up, girl. Look down on the world, it's a dirty place. Be sure to hold your head very high as you leave the room.

I stalked off as proudly as if I had made two hundred bucks at the Frog Market. I wouldn't be able to sell my T-shirt to anyone because I'd ripped ugly holes in it. The thing was my best one. So what? Life was an opportunity to buy a new second-hand sweater, wasn't it? Life was a chance to solve the hardest math problem and again get the only A$^+$. You'd have your coat wound around your head, hopefully this time the pair of pantyhose they'd tie you with would be more expensive than before. Well, they'd have to keep their noses out of it if they knew what I meant. I'd buy the foulest dog repellent spray even if I starved to death. I wouldn't care to be polite and understanding. The chap who planned to throw a coat over my head again would be very unhappy. He could take my word for that. Long live dog spray! Nikolai slammed the young man's image on the door under my nose.

Outside, as huge as the Balkan Mountains, Rosen waited, a bat in hand.

"Nick, shall I bump her off?" he roared, but the wooden door said nothing. Most probably, it was as dead as the Dead Sea. Rosen chucked the bat onto the floor. He clutched me the way Grandpa used to grab an armful of sticks before he sold the farm on account of the bad brandy at the *King and the General* pub. The hulk of a man dragged me to the hole in the hedge and pitched me onto the ground.

"Beat it!" he thundered.

I made a try to squeeze through the branches of the loathsome hedge. It was disgusting. I pricked myself on a dozen thorns. My trousers came apart and trickles of blood ran down from the cuts on my legs, arms and back.

God, let me invent you one more time. I want to pray to you. My limbs are drained of energy and I can't move. I wish you knew how much those thorns torture me. You know, of course, that I've made you up, but all the same, thank you for giving me strength, God.

I crept like a hearse carrying an old woman who died a week ago. What a quiet evening to collect any old crates I'd missed! I could have taken a drunkard to his poky place, and his wife would have given me hot soup out of gratitude.

Keep your chin up, girl. You've got fried rice at home. You'll put black pepper on it. Everything in the garden will be lovely. Life's a wood chip lodged in your back. You have to remove the splinter. It's up to you to let the wound fester, or you clean the sore and let it heal quickly.

I trudged down the bumpy lane, thinking. Where was the key to my little room? Where was my latchkey, damn it! I heard a small yelp, then barks and howls broke the long silence. I listened hard. The blaring went on endlessly, like a road to a graveyard.

Rosen was barking.

—⁂—

After Anna, the night smelled like a heap of old clothes, and the stench made my hackles rise. The whole town got on my nerves, all streets and faces reeked of a second-hand store, and the guys were second-hand fools, every one of them. The only place you could live here was behind the security wall — a solid, powerful structure, all steel and opaque glass. Our residence was within the guarded area, my mother's and father's home, in fact. The house that belonged to me, of my own volition, was built in the middle of a pine forest, which they created from scratch for me as they followed my step-by-step instructions.

Ten acres of spruce, silver fir, and seven other different types of pine trees — I don't give a tinker's cuss about the seven types of pine trees, but when duffers visited my official residence — oh, how they gaped at my pines! They contemplated my magnolias, going overboard on exclamations and full of praise for the man-made river they had carved out for me. I enjoyed its pure waters and clear, pounding rapids. It cost an arm and a leg. *A nasty thing!* In place of that phrase, I had used a swear word which my guests well deserved, but my literature teacher edited it out. My mother had hired the old cuckoo because she was a proud thing and wanted to be sure my essay had high artistic value. Water snakes bred in my artificial river. *A nasty thing.*

"We would like to behave appropriately like someone who is refined and sophisticated," the pedagogue said a wry smile in her face. To be honest, it wasn't all that pleasant. The water snakes were an infernal lot. I mean that my old man didn't fork out a million bucks to have a riverbed dug up in his backyard so I could breed water snakes, leeches and frogs in it. The fish died off like the cockroaches at school. My mother complained to the principal that roaches crawled on the classroom floors, on her son's sneakers, too, mind you, and she, Mom, had sponsored the school. Therefore, she often asked herself if she'd been pouring dough into a barrel that had no bottom at its rear end. The principal threaten to fire all the cleaners and they, clutching buckets filled with poisonous brew, exterminated the vermin within an hour. Mom, because she was striving to be a pillar of society, that very afternoon, poured more greenbacks into the same barrel, and the principal invited her to lunch.

Shit! The literature teacher didn't speak English or she would have edited "shit" out. The word is an exclamation, an offensive one, I focus on this fact for the sake of the less educated characters whose parents can't afford to pay for English tutors or private lessons. It was Anna who smelled to high heaven of disinfectant, an odor typical of second-hand marts, and she alone among us lived on the wrong side of the safety wall. She got A+s in all subjects, the idiot, but her exceptional grades also reeked of second-hand shops. She slipped on the same jeans three days in a row, and even uglier skirts on the following two schooldays. She had on identical blue denim shirts from Monday through Friday and wore the same pair of ankle boots even though it was already April. She polished them, but the shoe polish smelled of second-hand garbage, too.

I asked her out for coffee. For the time being, I didn't plan on taking her to my house by the man-made river where water snakes abounded. Sure enough, my mother went off the deep end on account of their slithering profusion, so the reptiles bit the dust the way the cockroaches did. However, frogs as fat as turtles multiplied quickly. I really hated it when frogs jumped everywhere. My mom refused to put up with their croaking and spawning, and the frogs, too, cashed in their chips. A guy with a mustache threw a container of fish into the river, then another container of bigger fish. Anybody keen on fishing is most welcome to come visit me. I'll let them use their fishing rods on my property for 200 bucks an hour. The snobs didn't come to catch the dumb fish, which the mustache guy kept hungry and the foolish trout bit the hooks like they were popcorn.

No, the morons visited me so they could brag later that they caught pike in Julian's river, and post pictures on Facebook of my *canal* and my summer residence. Mom was always expounding on how much dough she'd forked out for my place and how awesome it all was. There was no telling where one floor ended and the next one began. All the windows looked south towards my man-made river, the pike, trout and eels. Behind the house Mom had a team of carrot-crunchers plant cherry, pear, and apple trees. To be honest, I don't give a damn about fruits. I drink only freshly squeezed juice. The hicks brought in big conifers with lots of dirt around the damned tree roots, then a backhoe dug a trench into which they stuck the big trees. An unimpressive specimen arrived and within two days assembled an irrigation system.

An unintelligent woman, quite broad in the beam, came along to water my magnolias and jasmine shrubs to keep my landscape in good shape. Every time she caught a glimpse of me, the jelly-belly bowed respectfully. If she failed to do that, or didn't have a smile as big as her tubby ass on her unintelligent face, I'd fire her. They all needed to know who owned the residence, and who was a servant girl there. That was the way the world went around — some served the soup with crusty bread, while others ate the soup to develop a sense of responsibility and govern the world.

I am at the top of it all. I've taken the lead. I will lead them, all these idiots.

My math teacher, an obnoxious squirt, at long last came to the correct conclusion that he had to smile and bow to me. It was evident he had learned the basic theorem of life I taught him. If he didn't smile, adios, pal, no hard cash for you. A pleasant auntie tried hard to get me well-schooled in the art of diplomacy, creative writing, and poetry. She also learned her lesson. However, her radiant smiles gave me toothaches. I told her, "You smile unctuously, Madam. Quit it, or there will be no hard cash for you. Do I make myself clear?"

My statement put the auntie into a state of confusion and, as a result, she was beaming even more unctuously. Some folks are incompetent. This teacher of mine is the most intolerable gasbag among them. Mom pays her to edit the memoir I'm currently writing. I'd like to be televised and remembered as an intellectual and an author — that muck heap Nikolai Caramelitev, the gentle one, fired my ambition. He's as dumb as a bowl of cheap soup. I'm tutored in English by a Miss Magnificent, a real stunner, just forty-something. I invited her to my place. We fished and hunted frogs. She was quite good. She taught me a number of techniques in the sphere of skin and passion pleasures. I had used another phrase here, but that teacher, as barmy as a bedbug she was, edited my prose.

"Please, Julian," she gasped. "Please! Please! Please, let's maintain decorum!"

It's maintaining decorum that pushed things that far: towns, cities, the countryside and the girls smelled of second-hand stores.

"Anna," I told her. "You smell."

She said nothing. A screw loose that was what she had. Didn't feel like communicating with me. The idiot walked past me, didn't even look in the opposite direction, and it felt like she walked past a dirty window through which you could see nothing at all.

"You are stupid," I told her. She didn't respond. This crooked chick could make you think you were not all there, or even worse — you were going to buy the farm. You were convinced you were at the top of the world, but the truth was she didn't care. She'd already buried you in the grave destined for ignorant louts.

As we put the urine-soaked coat over her head, I pinched her sharply. I gave a fiver to each of the morons in my class to press down hard on her head and I pinched her wherever I pleased. I nipped her cheeks and squeezed her. I wished I could pull her muscles apart. I bit her and bit her and wanted her scraped skin to bleed. I used a felt-tip pen and wrote a letter on her stomach, which I had included in this memoir, but that lunatic editor, the teacher, deleted it. For sure, five years in the clink if a lawyer nabs that letter, so the lunatic described the situation for me. Of course, she said her piece in other oily, highfalutin words.

To learn English, I stayed in the three best places in London, two summers in a row. I flew to New York to pursue the same goal. Anna, the second-hand aficionado, had never set foot farther than Frog Market in our backwoods town and spoke English better than me, the dimwit she was. When she cackled in English, I couldn't make heads or tails of what she said. There was a girl, a friend of mine who communicated with erudite dudes. She lived behind the iron aluminum safety fence — it wasn't so much the fence, it was Road 109 I had in mind. The characters with cheap clothes and canvas shoes from the Second-Hand store didn't dare venture near our place. Anna didn't care about it.

Although rolling in dough, Mom and my neighbors got hopping mad when they had to pay the guards, guys with shaved heads and huge shoulders. The shaved heads wouldn't let a fly crawl on the grass in our walled community, let alone a lousy second-hand store geek creep into the property. The shaved ones had dogs and didn't even bother to beat the outsiders, the nerds, as I dubbed them. The huge shoulders forked out heaps of greenbacks for mutt-training exercises. In my opinion, a dog is smarter than a second-hand store fan. It was only natural the pooches left nerd carcasses in their wake.

I honestly thought my biology teacher had bats in the belfry. She constantly gave me a C. It was only natural Mom got mad; however, she bought this dumb pedagogue a car. It saved money in the long run. I didn't feel embarrassed when I showed the idiots my diploma, an excellent one it was. Well, the biology guru turned out to be a cutie. She declared she was convinced I had a formidable intellect. The biology broomstick smiled the way she should — *comme if faut* — as Maupassant, a writing enthusiast, used to say. My French teacher was about to cut off his (I didn't specify what the philologist was about to cut off because my editor, the moron she was, would delete the noun I'd prefer to use. We have to be polite.) — the poor educator tried hard to pound Maupassant's masterpieces into my head. His cake was dough through and through. So to sum up the situation, my biology teacher liked the Volkswagen car Mom bought her.

"Since earliest times, mankind has been fascinated by culture, but the individuals outside the safety wall remain in the second-hand store domain," the teacher preached. "They are evolutionarily dense and have limited mental capabilities. These so-called human beings cannot evolve because their brains remain locked into the algorithms of pork chops, sex, and alcohol. Higher humanity is evolving beyond Road 109. I'd like to focus on your own spiritual development as an example, Julian. Intellectually, you've taken a giant leap. Now, you are a wise young man."

I agree with her. The duffers behind my iron aluminum fence are similar to chimpanzees and cavemen who drew crazy things on cave walls, using bat droppings. Those wretches don't even know what a bat is. They're chicken droppings. Mankind is us, we are the clever folks. We have teachers who train us to take giant intellectual leaps. Of course, we'll do it the day after tomorrow. I don't feel like leaping today.

Mom has three Argentine tango coaches, a fitness personal trainer, and a couple of bodybuilding councilors — all these young men were handsome. She understood men. I had Mom track down who Anna's father was and check if the guy was a shabby clothes aficionado like his daughter. It transpired that Anna's dad was a splendid piece of work — the whole town rattled on about him. He'd written loads of bunkum, Mom said, and was famous, had an illustrious career etc. He'd talked on TV for two hours without a break. My mother invited him over to dinner. The dude did impress me. He drifted away into musings about what Shakespeare and King Lear thought of this or that, mentioned a dozen other writing talents — Balzac, Chekhov, Beethoven, Aristotle, quite famous and favorably commented about on TV. Anna's father told me, "You are a wonder-ful young man, intelligent and in possession of a brilliant mind. I am convinced Harvard will give you a chance to shine."

Mom covered some topics related to Harvard University, spoke for ages, and I didn't mind. Of course, you had to fork out heaps of greenbacks if you wanted Harvard, but a fat bundle was no problem in my part of the world behind Road 109. The writing talent was so polite! A question kept nagging at me, and it must have been stupid on my part, but I made up my mind to go for it.

"How's your daughter, Anna?" I asked him.

I was being cheeky, I knew it. I was poking my nose into the distinguished guy's affairs. With his face on TV all the time and Shakespeare on his tongue, the bard must have made friends with other big poetic wheels. In my mind's eye, I saw those guys glued to laptops as they put in writing one nonsensical verse after another. If one is sophisticated, however, one has every day to claw his way to a glamorous public image. Mom is very ambitious in this regard. Nikolai's mother, (a useful reminder: Nikolai, the pile of soft clay and a poet, is one of us beyond Road 109), made the writer do an essay dedicated to her, and what could the poor devil do? In the event of failure to write the piece, the bard wouldn't have money for a pack of cigarettes, no essay, no fee, you see. Unlike the mother of the soft clay, Mom was no bloodstained axe.

"Shall I hire Nikolai's private tutor for you, Julian?" suggested Mom. "She'll teach you grammar, poems and other language things. Within a month, you're going to be on TV."

If I have to, I'll write poems, I told myself. It should hardly be difficult. Nikolai had said poetry was a pain in the ass — (an *expe-*

rience in spirituality — that's how my ludicrous editor revised my phrasing), but altogether bearable. The girls are crazy about Nikolai now, both the second-hand empty watering pots and the chicks across Road 109. I think Nikolai is not crazy about women, to say the least. They don't deserve me, he was heard to say. Once in a blue moon, the young rhymer visits me, we discuss literature and I pretend he's great, the fragrance of his Santal 33 filling the whole house. It costs three grand a bottle. They say Nikolai's bodyguard is a bear with a sore head, gorgeous and tough. This hulk of a man could sing sweetly. Rumor has it Nick paid his minder to croon to him. And he, the bear, performed. He'd carol for two hours and a half, then gobbled down two slow roast legs of lamb plus lettuce salad, all the while spitting the bones on the floor, sporadically bursting into song. The only snag was that the bodyguard, for some obscure reason, at times stopped singing and barked.

"Anna," I said to her once. No one called her by her name. "The off-the-wall weirdo", the one off her rocker…She has no friends. She doesn't talk to anyone except Maria who like her is a fan of the lousy thrift shops. Anna sits alone at the double desk nearest the teacher and takes notes immediately after he opens his mouth. You could explain this — she doesn't receive private lessons and has no private math tutors like you and me. She doesn't stay in London to study English there. She is a church mouse, constantly cramming for tests, exams and idiotic competitions. Why does she toil and moil? It makes no sense. The studious wench will remain in the second-hand store area of town for good.

Out of curiosity, I went to see how they ran those thrift shops. The saleswoman, her legs as thin as shoelaces, was immediately ready to have it out with me. I own an apartment, a small one, barely a thousand square feet, in one of the hideous grey blocks of flats beyond Road 109 where the moles live — that's what, for the sake of brevity, we call the inhabitants who molder away in their dwellings with a cockroach infestation. That's where I take the mole women. I bought the apartment with my own money. Mom doesn't know about it. That saleswoman turned out to be skillful and knowledge-able. A brazen gal. She hinted she had a kid, but I made it clear I didn't give a hoot about it. Her husband was in Spain on business. I couldn't care less what he does after his daily grid, I said. If one of these days I get bored, I might take the brazen mole to the crummy apartment. I might throw her a fifty-lev note to buy cheese and two big steaks. Yes, I would. Soon I got tired of her and said, "Beat it."

She bowed before she made herself scarce, smiling almost as widely as she should — *comme il faut*. To get hired as a shopkeeper you have to bow — even in the second-hand store zone.

I loved it.

"Beat it!" I repeated. I did like the way she disappeared even before I counted to ten. *Comme il faut*, as that writing colossus Mau-passant from France or Belgium — I'm really getting mixed up on this point — used to say. A nice piece of cake, that mole, even if she was a saleswoman beyond Road 109.

"My daughter Anna is a lonely soul," began the intelligent poet or fiction writer, her father, as we watched TV. Even Mom had remarked, "The literary critics say he is the cream of contemporary Bulgarian literature." Okay. Then how come Anna is a crackpot? The writer spoke like somebody's got him on video — no stammering, no humming and hawing, no hesitation. I could feel this very private man rarely did interviews. Mom was looking at him the way Voltaire, our fox terrier, ogled our neighbor's English bulldog and wanted her right there and now. The writing talent didn't explain his views on Anna's talents or weaknesses. He kissed Mom's hand instead, and launched into some dumb poetic piffle. At this point, that clodhopper, my editor, erased "piffle" and wrote a "magnificent ballad" dedicated to Mom's hands.

Mom had a meltdown, got all fuzzy and teary-eyed, and invited the famous poetic titan to some little mystic place. I wasn't that slow on the uptake and immediately suspected her of having, like me, a roof over her head for exquisite occasions — as my clod-hopping editor had put it. I don't remember what my own choice of words had been. She, the stodgy burr, had deleted it.

"Anna..." the cream of Bulgarian contemporary literature began a load of mysticism in his sweet voice, "I don't see her too often," then he enumerated the elite universities he'd given lectures in, elucidating the essence of his artistic endeavors: Paris, Munich, etc. Mom had another of her meltdowns and asked if she could give him a lift to his native town.

The genius said yes; however, it would be better if she left him in the city center where he would be meeting another luminary of modern Bulgarian literature. They were going to discuss something to do with I don't know what. Mom was a washtub of warm rose oil that had spilled on the floor at his feet. The lyrical individual kissed her hand and, in a jiffy, turned out another poem for her little, or maybe middle finger, I'm not sure which. I think Anna's face resembled his, although she stared at you like an ox, while this rhymer here glanced over his shoulder like a sheep. I guess that was why Mom became as soft as curds. Apparently, she liked it when a sensitive guy contemplated her with a smile like that on a sheep's face.

I tried my luck at putting out the bait. "Perhaps Anna would like to come and visit us." Mom used to advise me — "Seize any opportunity that comes your way. Don't whimper. Or we'll be talking about a chance gone begging."

"Anna doesn't like accompanying me," said the stunning bard. "She has a life of her own."

The fact Anna was the poetic bloke's daughter made Mom's heart as generous as chewing gum stuck on the bottom of a chair.

"Why don't we invite your girl to our place?" she asked, and smiled so broadly that you could see her small intestine through her mouth, and maybe other intestines that weren't that small.

"I don't think it's a good idea," our guest muttered meaningfully. "She's focusing on natural science, and is not inclined to socialize with friends."

"She'll love it," insisted Mom. At that moment, I knew she was a great lady. Well done, Mom. You're magnificent.

Mom invited girls for a drink, especially ones who in her opinion met my needs intellectually. To be honest, she handsomely paid two psychologists to pick out suitable chicks for me — belles that not only lived on our side of Road 109 but also felt a longing to throw themselves in my arms. A load of nonsense! The mademoiselle Mom had selected was as fat as a kitchen stove, taller than the Bulgarian national bank building, and only talked about Chanel No 5, Armani, Versace, or Louis Vuitton bags. The large femme herself lead me to the room Mom had providently instructed our housekeeper to stock with clean sheets, coffee, gluten-free pastries, venison, and 0.5% fat yogurt.

I'd rather write three poems, ten short stories, even a novel, but I refuse to communicate *on an organic level* — look at the expression my deranged editor has barfed up and how she has suppressed the truth! Organic level my foot! Those kitchen stoves and Chanel No 5s weren't any good. You can't make a silk purse out of a sow's ear, O, my God! Thank you, Lord, for our daily bread etc… that's the way priest Gregory trained me to pray as he gave me private lessons in religious consciousness. The padre charged Mom 300 levs an hour to enhance my grip on philosophy and ethics. Every time the name of our Lord is mentioned, you immediately say 'Thank you for our daily bread. And lead us not into temptation, but deliver us from evil. For thine is the kingdom and the power and the glory forever. Amen!" I saw the simplified version on the internet, so now I just say to Our Lord, "Forever and ever Amen", and have no problems with Him.

I put in a great deal of effort with respect to the chicks inhabiting our side of Road 109, so no one could contend that the *pampered moron* i.e. me, had sailed over to the other shore (I had used the noun *pansy*. Here again, my clodhopping editor's passions for linguistic purity ran high. She's blocking my original artistic voice, the halfwit she is). A day before I had a date with one of those Mademoiselles Mom had picked out, I needed to go to the hospital to give Mom a letter from Doc Shom. This medical document confirmed that I had a nasty rash that produced a milky white discharge. Therefore, I could not see the young lady in the afternoon. Better throw myself under a subway train or write poems like Nikolai! Suddenly it dawned on me why he, in the first place, had started scribbling sonnets and things. It was because of those pancake girls our mothers served to us. Still, every once in a while — at least once a month — I had to close my eyes and (here the editor, the foul dragon, had revised and rehashed my memoir) sacrifice myself in the pancake's arms.

The fattest belles grumbled the least, so I'd pick an obese girl, stick it out for fifteen minutes, and did not even say, "Get lost!" as a true alpha male would express himself. I would kiss her hand, as Monseigneur Ivanov, an expert in acceptable conduct towards the opposite sex at social events, had taught me, and only then would I kick her out with, "Until the next time. Bye!" The fat pancake would zip up her bag, smiling from ear to ear. Mom was delighted that I hadn't sailed to the other shore like so many of my pals on our side of Road 109 had done. For instance, it was rumored that Nikolai landed there long ago and listened to his bodyguard's songs for hours on end.

Unfortunately, Anna was the daughter of the literary genius who knocked Mom dead, an occurrence that is exceedingly rare, I swear. Her eyes were out on stalks every time she saw him. Mom's able to extract big bucks from the bones of the dead before the Christian era as well as from the wind that whips up dour crones' skirts. Mom used to strip my dad down to his underpants to discourage financial evasion on his part, then give him pocket change — an amount big enough to get drunk once at an expensive restaurant, or six times at a cheap one. In a pub across Road 109, the poor bugger could drink for an hour and a half every goddamn day of the week. Mom is not a jealous woman. She's made numerous statements on that matter in my presence.

"If your dad tells me he wants a divorce, he'll get one within twenty seconds," she claimed. "In twenty seconds, I will marry an athlete two years your junior, son, if I feel like it. But why should I get married a second time? There's no need to buy an airplane if you're a once-a-week commuter to Paris. You just get yourself a Priority Class ticket, or rent a private seaplane. It's more practical that way. It's also advisable to book a Category A+ helicopter to go on a day trip to the seaside."

Wasn't Mom right! But then why did she choose such female alligators and whales for me? If you met these elephantine entities, you would sail to the other shore of your own accord. But I couldn't say this to my mother's face, could I? She'd deprive me of my Mercedes-Benz AMG SL, and probably kick me out of my own place, where she had carved out a river bed for me. On 3 May 2024, she was starting to build a helipad.

She'd buy me a small helicopter to start with if I agreed to her request to commence writing poetry. Hell, as I contemplated that gorgeous bard whose poetic skills had taken Mom's breath away and turned her on like an electric bulb, I said to myself, why not get with poetry? They put you on television. Chicks admire your sonnets, ballads, etc. I had an idea — I might pay Anna to write me a poetry piece or two. She's always hungry, and has a decidedly down-at-the heels appearance. But why doesn't her father lay something on her? Probably the guy's not her birth father. There's something fishy going on here, as Mom says. Nikolai owned a helipad and had a rather large helicopter, a hippopotamus getting airborne. The poet and his bodyguard flew it and the bodyguard barked. Damn it! That was what that sheep-headed editor had written. I'd used another phrase, but she'd deleted it, *I hope I would not hurt her poetic dignity or editorial pride!* (the sheep-headed educator's correction again).

"Anna sits in the first row, in front of the teachers. All by her-self," I continued cheekily looking her writer father in the eye. "I sit behind her. She doesn't talk to me, practically, doesn't speak to anyone. Please, Sir, tell her not to be afraid of me."

Wasn't I a blabbermouth? Talking the rhymer's ear off and stuff. He gestured soothingly at me, and pulled out a wad of banknotes. No less than five hundred, I surmised, judging by its size and mass. He said, "Young man, please give her some money. We've had a row lately over a certain matter."

"Hasn't she got a mother?" asked Mom pointedly, and I sank waist-deep in the carpet with shame. "Girls usually don't keep secrets from their moms."

At this point, the brilliant versifier announced that his daughter had a deep affection for her mother, but *alas!* Once a guy starts wrapping himself up in *alas* (I'm itching *to hurt his dignity and pride* — my sheep-headed editor's contribution again!) he wouldn't say a word about Anna, and Anna's mother interested me as much as our kitchen maid Tamara's dirty socks, pardon the ugly phrase I'd used. I didn't like Tamara not because she was old; with respect to *communicating with her on an organic lesvel* (another of my editor's follies), Tamara was Okay. I learned a lot from her, but obviously, she stuck her nose where it didn't belong. Expensive jewelry went missing, Mom fired her and explained to me that shortly after the theft Tamara popped down to the trauma center. She needed a cast to restrict the movement of her broken bones of the right hand. I wondered who had paid to have those fingers smashed.

"Does Anna have a boyfriend?" I asked. My mother was by no means taking the steam out of the sticky situation. She'd put her hand on the poet's knee and left it there. That was what the girls on our side of Road 109 did to me, but Mom wasn't a girl anymore.

"Can I invite you to *Turandot*?" Mom asked the poet. When things don't go her way, she invites the guy to *Turandot*. The rhyming talent didn't bother to shed any light on my question if Anna had a *soul mate*. (My country bumpkin editor!). As if I didn't know, Anna *wandered lonely as a cloud* (my moronic editor!) with her mug stuck in a textbook. Mom and her gorgeous lyricist humiliated me, and I hurt the dignity and pride of all their relatives in alphabetical order. I felt rather uncomfortable. I had the phone numbers of twenty-one young pancakes selected by Mom so they could exert influence and develop me in a manly and spiritual way. If I called one of these dolls, no matter who, the roly-poly peach would come running to my room within thirty minutes. However, I was allergic to them all and could hardly breathe in their presence. So, I sat in front of my laptop as useless as a crushed Marlboro box. No kidding. I felt blue.

"Anna," I typed on the laptop a week ago, "Anna, I care about you. I don't care about anyone else. I don't know if you understand me. I'm waiting for the damned night to be over. I'm as hot as a bowl of boiling soup. If I buy you some roses, will you come have a coffee with me? Nothing else. Just a cup of coffee." Gosh darn it, I'm such an idiot, Anna. The other day you were absent from school and I blew a fuse. I didn't feel like eating or talking. I walked past your shitty one-room flat. Plaster was peeling off the walls of your building. Your window was dark. She might be dying, I thought. If she's not at school, she must be dead. I called you. You didn't pick up the phone. Your father didn't say a word about how you were. I'll wring his neck. A *person of low intelligence,* that's what your father is! (That ewe, my editor, again. I'll hurt her dignity and pride all over the place!) Anna, I'm crazy about you. You can marry me if you want.

O, my God, I know no such things as gods exist, or if they do, they have bigger fish to fry. Not me. What a sentence did I generate, why don't I shoot myself right through the heart? I can't stand this anymore. No one understands me, except the manly girl who's lost over Anna like I did. The manly gal and I smoke together in the men's room and complain to each other that Anna has walked out on us both. Well, don't talk the talk if you can't walk the walk. Anna doesn't notice us. She's not all there. All her brain cells have shifted toward madness.

"Mom, can I talk to you?" I asked. She said she couldn't spare a minute because, right then and there, the handsome bard was kissing her wrist and reciting one of his fat poems to her. He knew nothing about his daughter, though. His daughter smelled of a second-hand store like a hearse for the dead. The lyrical squirt's shirt alone cost at least four grand.

"You can't talk to me," Mom repeated, cutting me like a cucumber. She's been flickering, an eclectic bulb about to fail, every time the poet used the noun *passion*. Passion my foot!

"Mom!" I croaked at the risk of losing the house, the garden with the artificial river, the helipad, the car, my ski vacation package in the Alps, and the swimming camp on Rhodes Island, Greece. "Mom, can you put Anna, Mr. Eustatius's daughter, on the list of the persons you recommend for my spiritual development?"

"Get lost!" she hissed.

A horrible, mean woman! That's how truly she cares for her son. She cares as much about me as about a leaky toilet. A venal creature.

A vicious one. I was sad. No one understood me. The rhyming stud was kissing my mother's fingers and scattering around spate after spate of rotten poems. How could my mother look so dumb? I'd never seen her ogling somebody like that. I left the room, but the two lovebirds didn't take any notice. I walked to the man-made river. The frogs had vanished into thin air and none were hopping; those environmental service cretins should have left at least a couple of tadpoles in the mud. How much had Mom coughed up to have the toads bumped off to the last croaking throat?

I stumbled over the helipad.

I had to see Anna. Naturally, I had the code for the hydraulic gate installed in the fence. I chose to drive my smaller car. Anna wouldn't stand me if I started getting uppity, a balloon blown up, that's what you are, she said. I didn't care a bit. My little car was appealing to the eye. A nasty wind was blowing, and I hated it! I couldn't ride my powerful motorcycle, damn it. So, I'd drive my Nissan Compact.

...It's like I've been thrown into a physics textbook — onto the wrong side of Road 109 — a pack of stray dogs chases my car and barks so loudly the paint peels off its fenders, and the headlights stop blazing. Three guys refuse to budge an inch as they argue in the middle of the street, or shall I describe this roadway as a series of potholes and craters? The blocks of flats are dark, although it's only ten-thirty in the evening. The streetlights have gone out, somebody's bawling and screaming, plus music blares out of three or four windows, and a couple of mongrels and an ambulance are waiting in front of a battered building. The non-stop drink shop is open, four characters swig beer, smoke, and play cards.

How come that fatuous poet twists Mom around his little finger?

Anna's block of flats was a five-story affair. A notable exception — the streetlamp on the nearby pillar wasn't broken. The front door, lucky for me, *was* broken, not that I didn't have a key. She lived on the top floor, in one room, no balcony. She'd never invited me to her place. Often on my way to Road 109 — o, come off it, every night I waited with the mongrels by the non-stop drink shop and watched her window.

It was sheer lunacy on my part.

My dad was the same make and model of a man as me.

"Julian," he would tell me after he had a couple of brandies, "I loved a girl. She was seven years my senior. Your grandmother said, 'Ditch her!' and I ditched her, Julian. But it was a big mistake. That mistake is still going on, Julian. She has a son your age. I go and stare at her window. This is stupid, Julian."

I climbed up five flights of stairs as energetically as a cockroach with a torn-off leg. The closer I got to the fifth floor, the cockroach lost more of its legs. Finally, I made it to the end of the staircase. The sign on her door read "Anna Eustatius ". I pressed the doorbell, although I knew — it didn't work. To hell with it. What would you expect from wretches like Anna and her dad Eustatius? To have a doorbell that rings? Go hang yourself! I knocked on the door like a well-mannered man, and like any well-mannered man I got no answer. So I pounded on the thing with my fists like a less cultured man, and getting no answer again, I kicked the damned thing like a genuine Bulgarian would. The door squeaked as if someone was withdrawing its bolts.

Anna showed up in the faded flannel shirt she wore in school. The place smelled sour — baked beans or lentils gone bad, or was it a twenty-second hand store? A dead man — that was what this poky flat smelled like. I haven't seen a dead person so far, but I'm sure a corpse would stink just like that — like Anna's blue flannel shirt.

"Come on!" I winked and pulled out two hundred bucks. Why did I do that? That's what you say to a pancake who's so oily and broad in the beam that you can't even look at her, let alone *court her* (my moronic editor's contribution again!). Then that door closed. The wood was eaten away by moisture so badly that if you kicked it, the thing would disintegrate — that poor door must have been white, but the white paint had peeled off and you saw a layer of brown paint under it. The brown layer was peeling too, and under it, brown, green and yellow patches glowed. All those layers of thin paints slammed under my nose.

"Anna!" I shouted as I banged the door down. No response. Nothing. She must have died inside, but of course she hadn't. The smell of lentils that had been creeping under the mold-encrusted floorboards could suffocate me. The light faded. The staircase went blind.

"Anna!"

I kicked the door. Lights began to creep out from under the other two moldy doors on the cement stairway landing — slowly and fearfully like the hungry dogs outside the entrance.

"Anna!"

Surely, those inquisitive neighbors were peering through the peepholes, but if they showed their faces, their inquisitive heads would go to the dogs. No man turned up. I used my knife and scratched a word on the layers of paint that had flaked off so badly you couldn't tell if they were paint or flakes. The teacher who edited my phrases and whose mind was that of a beef tapeworm deleted that word from my memoir.

Anna.

I wrote another word, and another, and another, and I dug with the knife, I carved with that dull knife into the peeling door. I cut out the sign that read **Anna Eustatius**. I kicked the door and it broke in two right where Anna Eustatius's name was nailed. Where was my lighter? Where? I had to set that shitty flat on fire. I'd cremate her blue jeans. Her stinky flannel shirt would be reduced to ashes. I didn't have a lighter.

I left that foul-smelling staircase. I went off with my tail between my legs like the dumbest dog in the world. 'Are you stupid?' I asked myself and answered, 'Yes, you are.' That was the truth.

I wanted to come out into the open and I did — after a hundred years, might have been two hundred. I crept out of that stinking block of flats. There, on the fifth floor, her lamp glowed like mad. That lamp on the fifth floor shone and shone and shone. I walked to my tiny Nissan car. By these shabby buildings, my automobile looked like a Samsung Galaxy Z Fold3 5G phone stuck in a basket of rotten pears. I passed by her block of flats and on the wall of the next building, an even uglier and more decrepit one, I scrawled with my knife, "Anna is a brainless imbecile".

Fool that I was!

—◦◦◦—

She had given him the money back without even opening the envelope. His daughter had stuffed the banknotes into a crumpled bag and mailed it to him at the house Kalina Kal had bought Eustatius when she was alive. Kalina was old, lovely, and her heart was weak. In a way, she reminded him of his wife — after a thin smile, Kalina would drift away. Perhaps she dropped in briefly on death and prolonged these visits with each passing day. When she died, Eustatius was sad, yes, intensely sad, but a man is not born to grieve. Two days after Kalina's demise, he met Milena, the mother of that awkward adolescent. This frenzied boy pig-headedly questioned him about Anna, his daughter. Anna had firmly refused to move in with the awkward adolescent's mother. A strange bird, Anna. "She doesn't talk to her classmates," the boy had remarked. A girl in Anna's class, a flamboyant and self-confident mademoiselle, had sought Eustatius out.

"You're a mean bitch," the girl had said to Eustatius. "I like her. I love her."

"Maybe my daughter has mental health issues," Eustatius had suggested. If he could remove one thing from the world, it would be the criminally insane. He feared for Anna. He'd given her so much sadness after her mother was gone that sometimes he wished he could put an end to his life. Eustatius remembered the night he had eaten sand. Anna, his wife — he had named their daughter after her — was his chance to get back to normal again. He had ruined it.

Eustatius had to slowly climb five floors to reach his daughter's place, a single room as wide as a nail clipper case. Eustatius's childhood days were bitter and lonely here. Cockroaches and ants that crawled on the window sometimes drowned in his cup of tea. He had worked hard as a porter to buy a pair of jeans. He had refused to go to school in the trousers his mother had made from his father's old pants. He'd put on his new jeans, his mother saw, and did not let him eat dinner for one week.

"We don't have enough money for bread."

Then Eustatius happened to like a blue shirt — as much as he liked Anna. It was warmly blue. For a month, he worked as a construction laborer, and had just collected the money when his mother said, "We need it for a bag of rice and your father's medicines."

The medicines did not help his father.

If Eustatius had bought that shirt, his life would have been different. He'd wanted to become a drummer, a banker, a dancer. He wanted to win a Nobel Prize in literature. His mother took the money he'd been saving for the shirt. On the following day, Eustatius visited that fat girl in their class, Erica. She let him stay in their luxury villa. There, Eustatius moved into the brightest and most elegant room, and massive as a submarine herself, Erica brought him food — meat, fruit, vegetables, vitamins, everything. Erica bought him the blue shirt, the most expensive pair of jeans in Bulgaria, Erica cut his hair, shaved his beard, put socks on his feet, massaged his back, and cleaned his ears, but she knew nothing about *One Hundred Years of Solitude*. She thought Kafka was a famous football player.

Anna.

Eustatius saw his future wife Anna clean the toilets, Marquez's book tucked down the back of her pants. Anna was in charge of the bathtub, which only Erica's father used and no one else, on account of the fact that the man suffered from hemorrhoids.

Eustatius could see the girl pore over *The Selected Poems* by Federico Garcia Lorca as she waited at the bus stop after polishing the tiles in the hallways and extracting the dust packed between them with a toothpick. He said to her, "You read a lot. I will become a writer because of you."

Maybe she fell in love with him too, but this sounded highly improbable. Anna remained cool even in the scorching furnace of summer. She was made of air that turned to steel after you breathed her in, but you prayed she wouldn't go away.

Fat Erica tied a rope around her own neck. She had seen what Anna and Eustatius were doing in her own room. There, on Eustatius's recommendation, the fat girl had hung Gabriel Garcia Marquez's portrait painted in oil. Eustatius's reaction was lightning fast — as a result of which Erica survived and threw out the rope she'd tried to hang herself with. She begged him on bended knees to forgive her, and fired her serving maid Anna. The heiress was awfully sorry for this, too.

Much love had been burned to a crisp between Eustatius and his wife, Anna. It was scary to love someone so much. An infant conceived in a night like that would not be normal. Perhaps Eustatius's daughter was barmy as a bedbug because he had prayed to that fictional presence the uneducated called "God" that the worm would not come into the world at all. May she be born prematurely and perish like so many premature babies. He had prayed so hundreds of times. But the little one had clung to her mother the way a tapeworm clung to its host's bowels. Her birthweight was 6.6 pound, her skin looked white and as delicate as spider's web, and her eyes were black. Eustatius didn't know why, or where his prayers had gone crashing. This package of spider's web had suddenly become dear to him — the sprog had survived because Eustatius was coolheaded and normal. It was not her mother's flightiness that helped the baby find its way to life.

When his wife's kisses left Eustatius and went to Gabriel Garcia Marquez, he was jealous of *One Hundred Years of Solitude.* He had told Anna that he would become a writer for her sake. Literary magazines began to publish his short stories. His novels were adapted for films. Stellar reviews poured in, written mostly by women whom Eustatius allowed to buy blue shirts and tailored-fit trousers for him.

"A load of old twaddle, all your work," his wife said to him.

He hated it, but he couldn't get her out of his system. She had bought him no presents. Not a shirt, not a handkerchief. She hadn't cooked for him. Her words, her smile, her terrible love felt like a planet turned to dust. Her touch was frozen fire. That was why their daughter had always been odd. Didn't talk to a single person in her class... Eustatius remembered that weird girl who, red in the face, had bawled and blubbered, "Anna-a-a!" His daughter had flatly refused to move in with this classmate of hers. The classmate's eyes were nails that stuck out and waited to be hammered down. And Julian, another classmate who admitted he had broken the door to Anna's dingy flat. Julian's mother and her admiration for Eustatius's books, none of which she had read.

Eustatius was climbing the staircase to the fifth floor. His father popped off on his way home. A neighbor found him dead and cold. In his lifetime, he'd been a quiet man, a stonecutter and a good hand at tilling the land. He had told Eustatius one thing, "I believed I had a son. Now I know I don't have one."

Eustatius still felt bad about refusing to go to the old man's funeral. He had said he was to speak at a literary festival in Brussels, or was it in Zagreb? He found out they'd left him only one jacket, old and shabby, the one his father had worn on the way home from work. Eustatius's daughter had sold her Grandpa's other clothes at the Frog market.

From Brussels, Eustatius bought her a bag and a T-shirt. His daughter didn't say anything. She took his gift, went out, and an hour later came back with a thick cardigan of synthetic yarn as hard as a sword and a ten-lev note. The garment was so stiff it stood on the floor instead of falling onto it.

"Put it on, Grandma," she turned to Eustatius's mother, then produced a chocolate bar from her pocket and divided it in two. She gave one half to the old woman, the other she ate herself. To him, Anna gave nothing. The girl left the ten-lev note, crumpled like an old shoe, on the table in front of the old woman.

"Buy some medicine for your blood pressure, Grandma," she said.

"I'm hungry, Anna," Eustatius had told her.

His daughter turned her back on him. She did not raise her voice. She did not lower it either — as if she had a piece of wire and not a voice in her throat.

"The restaurant is across the street," his daughter had said.

Eustatius was going up to the fifth floor. It was cold, and the windows of the stair landings were broken. The wind was blowing through the holes. While his mother was still alive, she planted geraniums and kept the pots on the stairs by the windows. She was crazy in a good way, Eustatius thought. Her geraniums had withered. The soil in the pots was baked and hard like paving stones. Apparently his daughter wasn't keen on flowers.

His daughter, Anna, and a burly man, his head shaved and smooth as a beer bottle, were doing something on the staircase landing. Eustatius quietly climbed another step and looked. The young man was installing a door to the bachelor flat. He was big, his shoulders seemed to begin in the decrepit block of flats and end in

London. The staircase landing was barely able to accommodate the bulging muscles of his chest. The thick red hairs on his arms glistened, the beard of the bull was thick, red, and scary.

"I'll give you ten grand if you marry me," the scary beard said to his daughter. "I don't live on *that* shore, you know. Sometimes I swim to it, but I come back. I love you," then suddenly the young guy, huge as the Himalayas, started to bark. The windowpanes rattled. The light bulb, black and dead the way Eustatius remembered it, burst into pieces. The hunk's barking was not only unbearable. It was venomous.

"Rosen, sing to me!" Eustatius's daughter whispered.

The tremendous growling sounds died as if someone had cut the giant's vocal cords. He propped the steel door against the wall and bent down as if he wanted to pick up something from the floor. There was nothing to pick up there. His red beard touched his daughter's hair — unwashed for at least a week, Eustatius thought. Surely the whale was trying to kiss her, and surely there was no hot water in the bachelor flat. Years ago, Eustatius's mother used to leave buckets of water on the windowsill to heat in the sun. She was a tough woman, his mother. Now his daughter did the same thing. Did she pour the bucket over her head, or take baths with cold water? Eustatius had bathed with his female classmates. Not with his wife.

The giant's hand, thick as a tractor tire, dug under his daughter's crumpled T-shirt. If Eustatius had a gun, he would have shot him dead.

"Sing," his daughter said as she pushed the hand that was trying to sift through whatever there was under her T-shirt.

Suddenly a voice as big as a storm spewed forth from the stair landing. It was a voice that had no end. It had no shore. A thousand eagles nested in it. It was an apricot garden laden with fruit, it was blooming trees and a kindergarten with a hundred smiling kiddies. A huge, deep, impossible voice. It felt like a blacksmith plated the whole shabby building with gold. It was the spring that came here and the sun stopped on the fifth floor. His mother's dead geraniums sprouted again. That was what the voice did.

Eustatius's daughter looked at the red beard, and for the first time in ten years, Eustatius saw her smile. Her smile was happy. Her black T-shirt was happy, too. His daughter stood on tiptoe. She kissed the man's hand, clammy, muscles and ugly red hairs all over the place. Eustatius said to himself, "She's insane." Yes. But what could he do? The song was kissing him too. The wild, thirsty, magnificent tune filled him, and Eustatius couldn't breathe.

She was again reading *A Hundred Years of Solitude*. Her room was clean, and the apartment was spacious and comfortable. All objects surrounding her looked expensive: a beautiful statue of a girl made of yellowish wood that made you feel a deep sense of relief, a discreet floor of the same wood, a writing desk, a computer, an ultramodern, confidence-inspiring iPhone, a coffee pot, a sofa, light-yellowish leather armchairs, a file cabinet made of the same sandy, nervous wood. The woman, not even pretty, left the *Hundred Years Of Solitude* and tapped on her computer then read her Facebook messages. A man, thin as the weakest mouse in the litter, came up to the woman, looked over her shoulder, and remarked, "You really did it. It's wonderful! You'll show them! I've never seen such a beautiful thing in my life."

A sculpture of a girl gleamed in the corner of the room.

The woman smiled at him.

"Please bring me some water," she asked.

The man shot across the sand-colored floor, his noiseless steps kissing the wood's fairytale depth. A moment later he returned with a crystal glass and a bottle of Evian water in a tray cradled in his hand.

"Anna," he began. "I hate it when you're not at home. Your presence protects me from the world. Shall we go for a walk? Look, it is warm and sunny outside."

The woman stood up. She was thin as a grasshopper, taller than the man, skinny like him. Apparently these two lived on a diet balanced to perfection, so healthy that surely they both would die in perfectly good health.

"We're not going for a walk," said the woman.

Slowly, like resin heated by the sun and gradually becoming soft to the touch, she began to undo the buttons of the little guy's shirt. The button on the left sleeve first, then the button on the right, at last her fingers, far from magnificent and not that young, focused on the shirt collar, a high quality cotton silk fabric. The short guy's round, almost wrinkle-free face beamed.

"Now?" he asked. "Our anniversary is tomorrow."

"Our anniversary is any time I like you better than I like myself," said the woman. Maybe she'd read that in *One Hundred Years of Solitude*, or she'd made it up. A person who read books on solitude came up with ridiculous sentences like that. "Solitude is our garment that exposes our essence as human beings," the woman added.

"Wait," pleaded the round face the woman claimed to like more than her own. She wasn't that pretty, the only ace up her sleeve was solitude about which she had been reading for a hundred years. Probably that made her desirable. No one had checked yet if that was the case.

The man put a ring on her finger, not a particularly large one, its diamond sparkling. No doubt the small guy's family name should be synonymous with surprise.

"Seriously Anna," he began. "If you hadn't come to the hospital back then, the linden tree Mom would have planted on my grave would be twelve feet tall now."

"'Maybe only six," the woman corrected him. His shirt had too many buttons — an unpleasant design defect.

"There's one more thing," the man added, and his feet pattered on the expensive floor, nippy as raindrops. Everything in this room was expensive, and that alone spoke volumes on good taste. The man brought a tiny box, which turned out to contain a superb pair of earrings. A necklace glittered in another box as befitted the moment when the woman liked him better than she liked herself. Logically speaking, moments like this should occur very often for there was hardly anything likable in that ordinary woman.

When the last button of the shirt had been released from its buttonhole, the diminutive gentleman took his turn with the buttons of the lady's velvet blouse.

The minute the event was about to occur, an annoying bell rang. The early warning system had been activated, and its electronic brain spoke in a human voice, "Mom, it's me. Anna. Please open the door."

The mother failed to look magnificent as she pressed a barely noticeable button on the wall panel. The electronic system lost its speaking skills.

The woman removed — slowly, with concentration on detail — the tiny slippers of the man whose life she had obviously saved, then, with deeper concentration, she took the sock off his left foot — first the elastic that had left a furrow in the gentleman's skin and sparse hairs, then, carefully, her fingers set his bare toes free. The sock, a fine blend of camel wool and Indian cotton fell onto the floor.

Near the magnificent room, behind the windowpane, an untidy figure showed up: a black T-shirt, black trousers, not slacks, jeans that were cut and shortened in the past, maybe at the time Leo Tolstoy, God rest his soul, wrote *War and Peace.*

The windowpane was clean. Despite its density, the glass let the voice through, a deep voice that had no color or fear.

"Mom, I need money. Help me."

The woman, who wasn't attractive, pressed a button that resembled a human eye. Exquisite aluminum — or perhaps a different material — blinds descended from the ceiling and rapidly touched the floor. They looked functional and expensive, these blinds, no exception to all other items in this house. The window closed its eyes. The black T-shirt and black trousers, probably sewn before Leo Tolstoy worked on *War and Peace,* drowned in the plastic elements of the blinds.

"Mom!" the blinds shouted.

The woman set the man's right foot free from the elastic, pulled at the sock then touched the smooth curve of his ankle. It was a slender ankle, weak and yellowish, or perhaps it was the wood floor that made it look so cheerless. Then her careful fingers released the pinky and the ring toe from the fabric. Finally the fine blend of camel wool and Indian cotton hid only the man's big toe.

"You save my life again," the man whispered. "Happy anniversary, darling."

The woman was proud that she had sculpted the statue of the girl in this incredibly light wood. She was proud that the chairs and the sofa, the floor, the sky on the ceiling in the sitting room, the wind and the stars in the bathroom were her creations. This woman had made a name for herself through her art projects and deserved all valuable objects that surrounded her.

"I love you, Anna," the man whispered, eagerly freeing his foot from the soft fabric of the sock.

SOMETIMES EVEN THE MOST difficult math problems could not cheer me up. The essay in English, and sheer exhaustion after running along the Struma River didn't help. The path, strewn with broken beer bottles and snakes under tree branches, didn't strike fear into me. I ran for so long that my muscles turned to a throbbing spasm, but I ignored it altogether. Sometimes, even though it was still quite cold, I would run five miles to the Chasm, which was what they believed to be a large swamp. I'd established it was a quagmire the first nine hundred square feet, then turned into a lovely quiet lake where water snakes bred and burrowed inside your armpits. This was the reason I called them armpit dwellers.

Now the water is cold. It feels weird when I go into the field, far from the slumbering town, after a long swim with the water snakes on my back. I am not scared. I fear nothing. The low noises calm me down, the packs of dogs know me well enough. I run again and again to the Chasm, the swamp or the puddle as they call it. It is freezing cold. My blood turns to ice, but when I get back home my thoughts are far from "those things".

This is only natural. I got top marks in biology, I won three biology competitions, and I know. But knowing doesn't help. I get so stupid that even after I've sprinted to the fifth floor, I have to throw on my sweater and go out again. It's dark, the wind pushes me, and the sky pours a thousand raindrops out of its ragged clouds. I'm freezing, but I keep plodding on towards Zoe's house. Zoe has become a significant boss at an insignificant ministry, and her son Rosen lives in her house. I know where I can find him — on the second floor. Their CRTV system is so rudimentary that I can block it within seconds. Rosen's mother is stingy, and skimps on new technology, the bungler she is. I can easily climb to Rosen's room.

I've read there are no side effects or health risks related to abstinence, but I think this is not true. Once I even climbed up onto Rosen's terrace — he wasn't there, must have been on duty somewhere. The second time I climbed to the second floor, he lay in his bed, barking quietly, so deeply and bitterly that I took to my heels and ran like the wind to the Chasm. I dived off a cliff. I swam. I swam hard and fast. The water was freezing. An ice crust thick as cream in a milk pot had begun to form. If you've boiled milk, you know what I'm talking about.

After swimming breaststroke for an hour, I had to break into a run and forgot to put on my sweater. I crept out of the Chasm and raced straight to Road 109. Then I scooted to the protective wall adorned with aluminum, then to the perfectly maintained helicopter landing and takeoff pad on Nikolai's property. I had to sprint past the mineral pool and the lake that was bigger than the Chasm. In this lake, no water snakes nestled inside your armpits. There was no mud to trudge through, and the shore was covered with golden sand imported from the Côte d'Azur or from some even more azure sea. I slunk unnoticed past the nasty thistles of the hedge, a few stuck into my back, but I didn't howl with pain. I advanced toward Nikolai's house instead. I was so cold I scrambled up the terrace under my own steam, and I couldn't explain how I did it without Rosen's help, even if my life depended on it. First, I climbed up the lamppost, a Japanese one, judging by the huge NIPPON sign, which stands for Japan.

I shinned up almost to the lamp itself. It was very difficult because the lamppost was as thick as a horse's neck. Finally, I sat down on the light fixture; as I looked around, I thought I had achieved the impossible, but the cold wind taught me otherwise. Carefully, for I could have cracked my head open, I stood up, my bare feet on the huge bare light bulb, twelve feet above the flower bed planted with flowers. I hoped the daisies and peonies would soften the blow if I slipped and came tumbling down on them. A distance of about five feet separated me from Nikolai's terrace, and I could see a lot of sharp stones on the path below, which I would be impaled on if I fell. On the terrace itself, unpleasant pots of flowers jutted out. I jumped up with all my might and caught hold of the metal railing. Okay. So far, so good.

Actually, it was no good. I was kicking in the air and trying to heave myself onto anything sufficiently firm to provide support. Rosen was sure to haul me over the coals again. He'd probably be happy if I broke all my bones on the pathway. Finally, gritting my teeth, I somersaulted over the flowers that bloomed in their unpleasant pots. I negotiated the bathroom window with ease and realized that the room had been transformed into a lavatory for the service staff. Long live that conscientious service staff, except for Rosen who had already given me a dressing-down for being impudent.

I had no time to reconnoiter or look back. Quietly, cautious not to wake up the bones of the dead, I dashed to Nikolai's room. What if he wasn't there? So what! I'd be waiting long enough.

However, Nikolai was in his room. The poet lay in a boat bed, his shoulders a pale yellow blotch by the light of a lamp with the familiar NIPPON inscription. Beside him, seated in an armchair, a NIPPON as well, Rosen the bodyguard waited. The leather furniture in this kingdom of peace and love looked yellowish like a bunch of dry roses. It seemed Rosen did not intend to behave like a wilted flower. He burst into song, and when the song died, he barked. Howling, he tucked Nikolai in. First, the bodyguard took care of the poet's limp shoulders, then concentrated on his belly and his arms, as weak as branches of a sapling.

Grandma and I had a linden tree. Grandma had told me she planted it when I was born. There was no room for it in our back-yard, so she dug a hole in the street and covered the seedling's roots with soil. The linden grew there for two years, then someone broke it, but it didn't die. It went on growing. I didn't die of bronchopneu-monia when I was two years old. Grandma and I watered that tree, I hauled a bucket of water from the fifth floor to the bench in front of our apartment block. A neighbor called Grigor broke the tree. He suspected it would cast a shadow over his kitchen window on the second floor. I thought the snapped branches now reminded me of Nikolai's arms that dangled, limp and thin, from his shoulders.

I'd been down with smallpox, mumps, and very often with sore throat. The linden did not die though. Grandma went off the deep and bought the most expensive cleaver from the local supermarket. It was a bad store— everything in it cost an arm and a leg. But Grandma was hopping mad, and didn't come back home before she procured the dangerous chopping thing. I waited for her, smoldering with curiosity like the garbage heap near the Chasm. I didn't know what my grandmother had said to Grigor, but he broke out in a yellow rash. She might have put a curse on him. Grandma could do it, she could all right, especially when she had kept mum for a week beforehand. When Grigor got better, he'd steer clear of both me and the linden tree. One day, the beanpole neighbor told me, "I'll boil your brain like a potato!" but Grandma dropped in on him one more time, and he broke out in another rash.

Rosen caroled. What I heard was not a human voice. It was a swamp with water snakes in it, broken linden branches, my folly which wouldn't let me solve math problems I liked so much, the cold air clinging to the boughs, the ice as thick as cream on top of the water — Rosen's barking couldn't smooth my ruffled feathers either. The wild, hungry molecules in my blood pushed me forward. If the giant kept on singing, I'd explode. I wouldn't waste time kissing Rosen. Mozart made divine music, folks listened to it in Salzburg, Vienna, Hamburg, and God knew where else. It was only Nikolai who listened to Rosen.

Nikolai did not move. He had closed his eyes. His brain must be increasingly befuddled — how could a man sleep while that voice was pouring explosions of lust and hunger into the universe? Then — even more quietly and sadly — Rosen let out a howl of anguish, dropped to all fours, and crawled across the floor towards the door. I looked at him, his bare back as broad as an airport, no belly fat, his arms, his elbows, his trim waistline, and his shorts that were an eyesore. At a certain point, the giant raised his leg, and I stood in the shadow, silent in my dirty T-shirt, which, though black, seemed to have accumulated more mud than the alley leading to Road 109. Rosen stood up and barked softly — a miserable little puppy, mourning for his mother who had allowed their master to sell him — and headed for the employee restroom where I'd sneaked in unseen.

I was watching him slip into his clothes when for a moment he turned to me. He'd got a word tattooed on his stomach, above the elastic of his shorts. It was a name. Anna. A thin strip of purple skin cut through his belly half an inch above the belly button.

Rosen walked down the stairs slowly in his expensive T-shirt. His red beard barked softly, his T-shirt barked too, and I thought Mozart must have barked like that, very quietly, probably only in his mind, so they wouldn't think he was not all there.

"Nikolai," I said as I tiptoed through the room.

He did not open his eyes, didn't look at me. My footsteps left muddy, shy patches on the floor. The bottom of his pajamas, discarded on the floor, looked like one of the dogs in the pack around the Chasm, a black mongrel. He'd bitten my leg. A cistern of blood gushed from the wound. I wasn't scared. I grabbed hold of the dog and beat him with a thick stick. I lashed him, I bludgeoned him, I hit his snout as hard as I could, and the stick broke. My blood mingled with the mongrel's blood, and ever since then, I could feel who wanted to punch my nose. No one could do it because I kept a thick stick in my mind.

My pants... my father inherited them from my grandfather, my grandmother made the pair tighter, and today I had struggled into them and dragged the pant-legs over my jeans because if you swam in an icy swamp you were very cold afterward. Grandpa's ancient pants landed on the fancy floor like the wounded pigeons that the stray dogs caught and ate up. I didn't care where my T-shirt had landed. I only noticed the bloodstains where the thorns of the damned hedge had clawed at my back.

Nikolai lay as still as the lamppost I'd climbed to reach the terrace. He was yellow and lukewarm. His hands didn't tremble. His fingers lay as motionless as the linden branches that Grigor, my neighbor from the second floor, had cut off with a saw. Nikolai's face was so beautiful it made my eyes hurt, so I stopped staring at him. I could have broken him into pieces or crushed his ribs. I didn't stroke his cheek tenderly. I had no desire to.

One day, when Grandma was still young, a baby goat died. I didn't stop scratching and stroking it. I kissed it, but it was as cold as the bowl of yogurt in the fridge. Grandma wrenched the baby goat from my hands and dragged me away like she was dragging a sack of rotten apples to the dump.

"You don't pet a dead thing," she said. "We'll skin it. And I'll make a hat from it, your new warm hat."

I burst into tears. To be honest, nobody cried or sobbed in our five-story apartment block, I had to learn this, and learn it quick. No more whining. No whimpering. I grabbed a handful of earth and stuffed it into my mouth. The dust dried all the tears.

"Okay," said Grandma. "You have to know that now the kid is happy in our Lord's house, and Our Lord gives you the goat leather for a hat."

Nikolai didn't stir, didn't even breathe.

No way.

I was in a hurry, so I tried to behave the way the water snakes in the Chasm did. They wanted to keep warm and shoved their heads inside my armpits. Not me, those molecules in my blood that conformed to the rules described in the biology books, they pressed and touched Nikolai, those silly molecules of mine. They weighed on the poet's chest. They refused to leave him in heaven where everything was pure and clean, and God sat by his side. Those hungry chemical compounds bit his skin. They pushed on, they insisted and pounded against his ribs. They drank his sweat and sank to the bottom of despair. I was fine. Biology couldn't explain why it felt so good and why my hungry chemistry felt hungrier. Nikolai tried to hide behind God. His dignity, or did they call it something else, slipped away. I did not let it go. Nikolai was quieter and colder than that baby goat I had kissed after it had died.

I let my molecules squeeze everything out of him. But could you squeeze water out of dry sand? They could. They turned the desert into a mountain brook that only I could see.

 It felt good.

I stood up. I did not look at Nikolai who lay weak in his powerless bed. It was no longer clean. It was messy and dirty, my blood and patches of mud all over the place.

"Hop it," he screeched.

The first time, about a hundred years ago, I left that room terrified, panicking before the statue of the magnificent youth. This time I was not terrified. I looked at Nikolai. My shabby T-shirt, torn by the thorns of the vicious hedge, and my wet socks were a sorry sight. He ran to our Lord for help, and I didn't mind. I said nothing. How could you talk to the beautiful face of a man who hid behind God's back? Then I noticed an interesting detail, a photograph taped on the wall above the bed. Both the devil and the angel are in the details. That was true all right. It was Rosen's photo, his head shaved, smooth as a box of ice cream, the rug of his orange beard bristling with rage at me. Another of Rosen's photos lay next to Nikolai's pillow.

"Hop it," Nikolai grumbled.

Not too creative, was he?

I had already sworn not to let anyone tell me to 'hop it'. I made the poet pray to Our Lord for protection. Before I left, I caught a glimpse of a pen on the nightstand. I felt like scribbling my name on Nikolai's pale chest, but I didn't do it. I wrote "I'll come again," on his shoulder.

—∽—

"Take all this," said the woman who wasn't even pretty. She got out of a giant-sized blue Volvo and handed a tall girl two bags of the kind that people collect garbage in.

A minute later, she was back in her car.

The girl, her hair coarser than the woman's, picked up the bags. She said nothing and didn't look at the impressive vehicle. It roared as a brand new Volvo was wont to do outside the confines of Road 109.

"Wait," the woman cried out as she held her hand out of the car window.

The girl's black T-shirt and black pants were large and billowed like mourning flags around her skinny limbs.

"Your father's partner is a very famous and influential woman," the lady said loud enough to be heard. The Volvo crawled obligingly beside the thin girl. "As far as I know, in the novel of your dad's life, Fernanda No. 2 is a page he's already deleted. Hey, this is also for you," an exquisite hand reached out of the car window, and a yellow paper envelope shimmered in the air. The girl didn't take the envelope.

"Your class teacher informed me that you scored the highest on the national math and physics tests," the Volvo lady continued. The girl didn't seem to pay attention.

She sat down on the ground where grass should be growing, but not a blade had survived.

The girl kicked off her left sneaker, part of a two-euro pair acquired from the Second Chance store, and pulled off her sock.

"Anna," the woman spoke evenly from her Volvo's cabin. The girl didn't seem to have changed her mind. She shook her sock and scratched her mud-stained ankle.

"Anna," said the woman. "I'd like to remind you that you should call me before you visit my house."

The girl pulled off the other sneaker. This sock was torn and her big toe stuck out of the hole like a traitor. It appeared that the right ankle was covered in mud as well, but the kid didn't attach any importance to that. She put on her sneakers, crammed the two muddy socks into one of the black bags the woman had given her, and walked over to the magnificent Volvo. She opened the back door of the car and chucked the black bags down on the back seat.

The passenger seat was occupied. A man sat in it, a petite individual, whose face made one think of an advertising balloon. The girl turned her back on the guy's good-natured face and the woman who was not that pretty.

"You're losing the game," the woman said as she honked her

horn. The new Volvo was a smart car. Its horn was provided with the option to sound to the rhythm of "A Little Night Music" by Mozart, or "Für Elise" by Beethoven; however, what musical composition had just sounded no one could tell.

"She's ill-mannered," remarked the good-natured face.

"Yes," agreed the woman.

She parked the car, got out, and opened the door for the small guy who slid out of the seat and, quite scared, looked around. Probably he had never seen potholes like the ones at the intersection of Summer Avenue and Levski Street. There was the most famous and well-stocked second-hand store, the Second Chance. The woman who wasn't that beautiful had heard about the dirt cheap goods available for sale there. Despite the low low-heeled shoes on her feet, she was a full head taller than the good-natured chap. So she bent slowly and gracefully — she always moved with grace — and kissed the man's lips. He smiled.

"It's a great pity," he said. "I've been looking forward to meeting her."

That day, love and understanding between them flowed as smoothly as an iPhone charger cable.

ZEUS WAS A RESTAURANT where no one would be ashamed to dine. The eatery was, of course, on the right side of Road 109 and had long become the stuff of legend in the public domain. Here you could safely celebrate your son's wedding without anyone bothering you. There was the option to order adorable creatures or be alone and crave solitude, which no doubt, was highly suspicious. It provided a welcome occasion to predict what would follow after your dinner at

ZEUS was over. No uneducated exclamations, comments, or sighs marred the atmosphere of the lavishly furnished eating institution where the waitresses spoke English, German, Spanish and French. Here the sculptures were carved out of wood the color of golden sand. The statues of gods the visitors had never heard of were too numerous to list, so discreet gilded plaques described who this god or goddess was and whom exactly they protected.

A dark blue Volvo pulled up in front of ZEUS; this elegant restaurant might have expected another, more convincing vehicle, but when a not-so-beautiful woman in a beautiful dress stepped out of the Volvo, everything fell into place. The Madonna in question had saved the restaurant owner's life. She had created all the sculptures within record time out of the wood described in the above paragraph.

A waiter in a dark blue tailcoat sprinted out to meet the lady who — if you believed the malicious rumors — had frequented *The Second Chance* at the intersection of Levski Street and Summer Avenue before ending up toiling away as a maid in the house of the Toreador i.e. the Bullfighter, the owner of ZEUS eatery. She had frequented worse places, to say the least, than the *Second Chance* store. A rumor had it she'd been dumped by a number of — let's not list here the names of the distinguished gentlemen. Oh, her heart had bled many a time! Anna-Barbara Vaughn's star started rising (actually the lady's birth name was Anna Ivanova) under the Bullfighter's roof. The Toreador, the petite man, was a financial planner or investment advisor; unfortunately, he was stricken with an obscure disease. His shoulders and knees started to swell, and if it hadn't been for Anna Vaughn who got his tongue swollen like a beer can out of his mouth, the Toreador would still be kissing Our Lord's slippers in heaven or the devil's boots in hell. It was unimportant where the Bullfighter was to end up, because he had enough money to remodel Hell and convert it into a five-star hotel. Another unusual thing happened that was the talk of the town — Anna-Barbara Vaughn's (actually Ivanova's) presence in the Toreador's room cured him. For a month, Ms. Vaughn stayed in Greece where she worked for an old-established family, which ceased to be a family after Ana Vaughn helped the husband, an emotional wreck, find peace of mind again.

It was rumored that the Greek husband's shoulders, knees, tongue, stomach, and feet started swelling as well. Anna Vaughn saved his life. She'd already saved the Toreador's life in a similar manner. The Bullfighter was a lonely and reclusive person who was lucky to find his only soul mate in the wide world.

A year later, Anna-Barbara Vaughn's genius made a brilliant display of its depth and perfection. Ms. Vaughn had dreamed of becoming a sculptor ever since she was a child, practically all her life. But who in this backwater country buried in provincial torpor could send her to study sculpture abroad? Her father was a stonecutter. He cut granite into pieces and built houses as uniform as the pumpkin seed shells he spat on the sidewalk. The buildings he left in his wake were sturdy, square eyesores with thick walls, veritable bunkers. The man was machine-gun fire. The windows of his houses were as wide as the eye of a needle. This remarkable character had a daughter, Anna Vaughn, and he loved only one woman, Anna Vaughn's mother, a pocket-sized thing, a speck of beauty in inverse proportion to her husband's imposing height. The belle made efforts to keep clear of the stonecutter. She cut potatoes into charming figurines, made clay dolls for their daughter, and carved human faces in tree stumps.

These faces looked peculiar, all puffy cheeks and hooded eyelids. The small figures she carved had swollen tummies, swollen knees, and ankles. All in all, Anna Vaughn's mother was not a charming person. Her daughter was not a gorgeous girl. Anna Vaughn's father stood no nonsense. No matter the guy doted on his wife, he often kicked up rows and quarreled with his better half. After every serious dispute, however, his legs, knees, stomach, or tongue would swell. Under these force majeure circumstances, only his wife was able to cure him.

What sort of woman is she, the stonecutter asked himself day in and day out. It turned out that their daughter also knew how to cure a swollen knee or tongue. Anna-Barbara Vaughn's mother still lived in that remote village of Kladni. At eighty-seven, she climbed hills with her goats and ran faster than the beasts. During his lifetime, her husband rarely dared to directly hurl insults at her because if he did, first his arms swelled up. The doctors warned his wife, "You'll need to dig him a grave, and dig it quick."

So even the old centaur, the stonecutter, thought that the petit speck of beauty, his wife, was adding something to his plum brandy or his bread, and when — though rarely — the two of them made the nice thing and love happened between them, the speck of beauty rubbed green ointment into his skin. Thus the stonecutter's limbs and tongue had no trouble at all. The guy didn't speak about the conclusion he had reached to anyone, and died, keeping his suspicions to himself. Long time before the stonecutter met his maker, he took great pride in his daughter: she toted a load of hardbacks and paperbacks around in a plastic bag, and while other kids got into mischief, she read books. He who mischief hatches, mischief catches, the proud father thought.

"She'll live and die an old maid," Anna Vaughn's mother presumed.

"The women in my family don't die old maids because their blood pushes them into looking for guys," her father pointed out.

"It pushes them all right, but most guys are no good," the stonecutter's better half said with an air of encyclopedic knowledge. "Reading doesn't put money in your purse. A woman must be able to deal with a swollen tongue or wrist," she added. "If you cure your husband of his swelling, he'll not only love you. He'll show respect and gratitude to you."

"What if the wife adds a thing or two to her hubby's meal… and the poor devil swells up?" the stonecutter ventured.

Within an hour and a half his tongue grew fatter and bigger. Unfortunately, right then his wife was out in the garden. Or maybe she reacted too slowly, a detail that would raise eyebrows if you shed enough light on it. Long story short, the stonecutter ascended to heaven to cut stones for the angels. They needed raw materials to build their palaces on the clouds and most probably looked for good workers. A stonemason would work his fingers to the bone both in heaven and on earth. An expert stonecutter wasn't expected to sow corn or teach English grammar for little cherubs, was he?

The old man was admitted to paradise, and there beauty blossomed and bloomed. But beauty was only skin deep. The stonecutter was born in Bulgaria, and heaven could not surprise him. On the contrary, the stonecutter asked the angels if in paradise they had granite as firm and beautiful as granite near the village of Kladni in Vitosha Mountain. They had? Weren't they pulling his leg? Come off it. They didn't have it. That was what the old man regretted most — he hadn't slipped a piece of Kladni granite in his pocket!

And there was something else in Vitosha Mountain, but only women knew about it, not the babes and the heiresses, but the grey and quiet wives, like Anna-Barbara Vaughn's mother knew it.

You could say it was a weed, that mauve flower, or was it a kind of herb? It made your flesh crawl and become puffy like a balloon, in fact your flesh grew twice to ten times thicker and harder, depending on how long the weeds simmered and what wood burned under your cauldron. And the mauve flowers struck roots in only two northern valleys in Vitosha Mountain. Drink mauve flower tea, and you'd melt like butter in a saucepan. Sprinkle mauve flower tea over your bread, and you'd swell up like a bagpipe, depending on how you dried the purple bunch, and if you boiled it over flames of pinewood or branches of a hazel tree.

"Your father's dead, Anna," Anna-Barbara Vaughn's mother had said. "Don't believe a word of what he told you when he was alive. Before he breathed his last, the liar fooled you into thinking you were pretty. You are not. The books you're reading day and night waste your time. Look around the town. Pick up a dumb man. A smart one won't look at you twice. If worse comes to worst, make do with a wimp or a cripple, so you can escape from him if you feel like it. You're reading again. You're reading! If you'd read enough to become a doctor, I wouldn't mind. Folks will be sick all the time. Nothing feeds a hungry doc's mouth better than pain. Pain puts the softest bread and the tenderest beef on a surgeon's kitchen table.

The distraught widow collected Anna Vaughn's books and burned them in the fireplace to boil wild pears and quinces. Anna Vaughn sobbed and bawled for days. Her mother did not give her anything to eat.

It turned out hunger was the best medicine for sorrow.

You grieved as much as you wished, but your stomach wanted food and turned a blind eye to sorrow. At first, Anna Vaughn refused to look at the mauve flowers that bloomed right next to the toadstools.

"Nothing puts money in your piggy bank better than fear of death," Anna Vaughn's mother said. "When a man's shoulder swells and pain starts, fear grows like your shadow in the afternoon."

Anna Vaughn's Greek husband swelled up like that. She inherited his big bucks, and humble Ana Ivanova became Ana-Barbara Vaughn. She, like her mother, carved potato figurines and sculpted faces in clay. You remembered the man after you saw the face Anna had produced. She, like her father, cut stones, but didn't sell them. She used them to make small sculptures instead.

"She, who has a heart of stone, makes stone men," remarked Anna Vaughn's mother. But when Ana Vaughn saved Toreador's life by pulling his swollen tongue out of his swollen mouth, Anna Vaughn's mother did not worry a bit. The female scion of the family wouldn't be wiped out, she thought. However, Anna Vaughn's mother didn't like her granddaughter. Didn't like her at all.

Anna, the granddaughter, read all the time and all the time kept mum. That was Okay, the young fool wouldn't talk through her hat, but her silence was an unkempt lawn where nettles went to seed. Her eyes were a bunch of mauve flowers, boiling over pinewood flames. That meant that the weeds would make the brain swell up, but you couldn't pull the brain out of a man's head. A guy's brain was softer than his tongue.

The old woman showed the mauve flowers to her granddaughter Anna, the dope who crammed for tests. She must have bats in the belfry, thought the old one. If she's not crazy, why does she keep putting on shabby black clothes? Aren't there white, blue or red rags in the *Second Chance*? In the village of Kladni that is as big as a sheep shadow, there's a second-hand store as well. They sell dirt cheap shirts and pants. It's just that young Anna isn't all there. Just like her father, the lousy poet. Poet? Come off it!

"You won't stay with this moron long," said the old woman when Anna-Barbara Vaughn — then a simple Anna Ivanova, a cleaner and char girl, introduced her fiancé to her mother. "Don't forget the flowers I showed you," the mother said as she threw a bunch of mauve weeds to her daughter. "You'll need them soon."

Now, Anna Vaughn participated in a number of international sculpture and art exhibitions. "Unique!" the critics wrote about her.

Anna Vaughn had a thing for plants. In each of her eighty-four pots, an unremarkable flower glowed. It bloomed only three days a year, in July, tender mauve petals. Thin stems. No scent, yet the blossoms drew the eye to their soft fire. So did Anna, the flowers' owner. Though not remarkably pretty, if Anna Vaughn made an appearance at a festival, all eyes were on her.

That day, the Toreador, so grandly named on account of his unspectacular stature, did not accompany Ana-Barbara Vaughn. The Maitre d'Hôtel — or, to put it plainly, so that the less educated of us would understand — the head waiter of the ZEUS restaurant, took Madame Vaughn to a small room with wonderful acoustics and armchairs that took the shape of your body. If the guest waved his hand, Vivaldi's *Four Seasons*, Spring, floated in the air, though Anna Vaughn was not interested in spring. The only time of the year important to her was the month of July.

After about ten minutes, a delay that prompted Ms. Vaughn to rise from her seat and prepare to leave the lovely acoustics of the auditorium complete with Vivaldi's *Spring*, she was confronted by an elegant individual, tall, fair-haired, blue-eyed, wearing an Emporio Armani suit, a Park Avenue tie, and a pair of Johnson and Murphy shoes.

"As always, I presume you don't have a penny to bless yourself with," remarked the woman who was not even pretty. "I will not buy you anything to eat. I will not give you anything."

"You look older," he said.

"Your false hope again," the woman said, "Okay, I need to talk to you."

The two sat down at a small circular table.

"Anna got accepted into Harvard University," the woman announced, "She's won a scholarship, but a part of the amount — a fifteenth of it — for her studies has to be borne by the family.

"You're the man in the family," the Armani jacket pointed out. "So you will provide the required payments, Ana-Barbara Vaughn."

The woman kept silent, her dark eyes, endless as the night before death, studied his face openly. Her gaze did not bend down or kneel. It flew where it wanted and did not apologize. She was carving her initials on the poet's skin. She, Anna Barbara Vaughn.

"I liked one of your latest stories. It focused on how hard it was for you to forget me," Miss Vaughn lifted her head, "Don't get your hopes up. You can't forget me. One does not forget pain."

Armani's right sleeve reached for and touched Anne Vaughn's arm.

Vaughn's face split into two halves, both sharp and silent as vessels full of acid.

"Your kisses on each individual finger and toe plus verses dedicated to each finger and toenail sound painfully familiar to me," Anna Vaughn said.

"I'd like to do it now," said the Armani suit.

The Maitre d'Hôtel brought Madam a tiny glass of Baileys.

"I'll pay just as much of Anna's expenses as you'll pay," said Anna-Barbara Vaughn. "Not a penny more."

"Anna Vaughn," said the man, smiling. "Your words bring disgrace to Anna I once knew. Anna, the only woman I've loved in my life."

Although Ms. Vaughn was not beautiful, she did not look bad at all. On the contrary, she had not put on weight, and her eyes were as sharp as before. She said:

"I accept the first part of your statement because it is true. We both have listened to the second part numerous times. It no longer holds my interest."

"I am not in a position to pay for our daughter's education," the Armani jacket said.

"Eustatius," the woman began as she allowed her eyes, dark as the pair of Johnson and Murphy shoes, to go for a walk around his face. He hadn't aged, the resourceful fellow he was. Time had gently caressed his body. Attractiveness was Eustatius's tool of choice to deal with difficult life situations.

"I suppose your uneducated female fans still besiege your hotel. They'll take any bait, your charm, and magnetism, I no longer care about," the woman spoke evenly. "When we met, you had scabies. 'These damned mites are killing me', you said back then. The poems you produce are a disgrace to literature. I wonder if it is pleasant to live as a lapdog, or, how shall I put it? Is it fun to behave as a kept woman?

I could use another, more expressive word, my dear Eustatius!"

The man stood up and adjusted his Ted Baker tie in a leisurely manner.

"I won't pay anything," he said as he turned to the door. "You knew it. You asked to meet up with me just to see how I looked."

"I won't pay anything either," said Ms. Vaughn. "My mother never helped me with money, and you should know — connoisseurs of art in Europe and America buy my work."

"Your mother is really obnoxious. So are you," whispered the man. "We could've been happy…" he added.

No. They couldn't be happy together. What was going to happen to his daughter? There were no flies on her. She was too smart for her own good. Sooner or later, smart women went crazy.

—⁓—

I RAN FAST. IT was cold, the wind hurled handfuls of frost at my face, but I couldn't stay in my bachelor flat with the old laptop I'd charged a classmate for the English essay I'd written for her. I had all types of students coming and asking a favor from me.

How much do you charge for a short essay? I wanna get an A in English, mind you! I didn't tell her the price in euros or Bulgarian levs. Give me a laptop, I'd accept a used one. Your old laptop will do the job, or offer me an iPhone. Your boyfriend's, your mother's or your father's old cellphone. The essays I wrote on which my clients got an A cost up to five hundred bucks depending on the subject. However, the teachers weren't born yesterday, and I knew I could rarely fool them. So in the beginning I wrote an essay on which my habitué got a B-, then slowly, with difficulty, a B+. , and finally, if the person was greedy and wanted a whopping A+, I'd toil and moil on it for days on end. My customer paid through the nose. I had to buy a prom dress, but I didn't care a bit because I wasn't going to any prom. Some of my classmates wore their sisters' old prom dresses or their brothers' black suits. Three second-hand prom dresses cost a B+ essay. I wrote one quickly enough and sold the gowns at the Frog Market. The stallholders knew me well. I did not demand more than the rag was worth. I never accepted less.

"Sixty," I said one day.

Stannoy, the burliest and meanest of the traders, crumpled the dress as he spat on his fingers before my very eyes.

"Ten," he grumbled.

I pulled the gown from his huge hands and walked away.

"Stop!" he shrieked, "Thirty. Thirty-five."

I didn't look back.

"Forty-five. Fifty. Fifty-five. Okay, sixty. Give me the rag."

"Seventy," I said.

"Bitch," he snarled.

"Eighty," I said.

He produced a bundle of twenties out of his pocket, counted three notes, and waved them under my nose. I looked him in the eye. At one point, he added another twenty. I snatched the money and chucked the dress down on the ground.

"Dirty bitch," he said.

At the Frog market, Grandma Nada sold hand-knitted socks, used jar lids, needles, old shoes, packets of cheap beans — two levs per pound. Sometimes I'd give her a dress, a pair of trousers, and she'd sell them for ten levs. It felt good when in the evening after school I shouldered her bags and carried them to her flat for her. Only once did I play hooky so I could get Grandma Nada's bags; she lived on the third floor, and their elevator didn't work. I hated seeing her bend to the ground like a fishing pole under the weight of a big carp, so I hauled the bags to her place. One evening, she made me some tea.

"Take a seat, Annie," the old woman said. "I'll have to let the tea brew long enough."

One Sunday, we cooked together, I had brought her potatoes. Her place had grown chilly, but it was warmer than my bachelor flat. I peeled the potatoes and removed the mud stains from the clothes she hadn't been able to sell. Sometimes in the evenings, when it was time to go to bed but I couldn't sleep, I popped over to Grandma Nada's. She told me about her daughters and grandchildren — the younger one in Germany, the elder in Germany too, but in another town. She showed their pictures to me on a phone as old as our apartment building, and I said the girls were cute, although their faces were small yellow spots on the tiny screen. How wonderful it was to have Grandma Nada talk to me, how wonderful! One night, inadvertently, such things hadn't happened to me so far, I blurted out, "Can I call you 'Mom Nada'? I'll call you that very rarely."

That evening, we ate the bowl of steamed rice she had cooked, and the next day I wrote two essays — one for a client who wanted a B+, the other one for a more modest classmate — a B- composition. I filled the fridge, a thirty-year-old veteran called Frost - with ground meat, cheese, peppers, and white bread. Grandma Nada saw what I had left in her miserable Frost, and a tear rolled down her cheek.

"Now, we have plenty of food," I said.

"Thank you," she said.

I was thinking of Grandma Nada as I ran towards the Chasm. I felt good despite the rain, an avalanche of freezing mincemeat and cutting wind. I swam in the swamp every night until my teeth chattered worse than laptop keys.

"Hey! Stop!"

No sane person wanders around a swamp on a biting cold night. Killers too stay at home when it's raining buckets, I told myself. The guy moving towards me was probably some petty thief. He looked as thin as a rail and had a bristling beard, black and thick. You could say that the night flowed into his face and vanished in it.

I paid no attention to him and kept running no faster or more panicky than before.

"Hey!" the black bristles shouted.

"If you touch me, I'll kill you," I said. I had a rusty penknife in my pocket, nothing else. I had never used the blade except to peel potatoes with it. "Go away."

Something heavy and warm landed on my shoulders. The stranger had wrapped his coat around me.

"I won't give you any money," I said.

"I'm not asking you for money," his voice was a water snake burrowing inside my armpit. "It's cold."

I threw his coat on the ground and moved on. The lunatic caught up with me, draped the coat on my shoulders again –the thing, as all clothes in these parts, smelled of *Second Chance* at the intersection of Levski Street and Summer Avenue. I ran quickly, the coat pleasantly warm on my shivering skin, but the dunderhead, the bearded kite, caught up with me.

"I won't give you your coat back. Write this down and read it in case you forget," I said.

He said nothing. Was it my voice that had him in stitches? His laughter was as big as the lake, full of pebbles, fish and sand — that was what the man was like. I found he was funny.

"What are you chuckling about?" he asked.

I didn't bother to answer his question. I ran up to the shabby apartment block, the first of three behind the bank, an eight-story affair with sagging plaster on walls all over the place. The bearded kite sprinted behind me.

"I live here," the kite announced. I threw the coat on the ground, hoping against hope it wouldn't fall in a mud-hole. Within a couple of seconds, the stranger again threw his coat over my shoulder.

"You're worse off than I am," he told me. "I'm giving it to you."

I tripped over a stone and was about to bury my nose in one of the many potholes on the road.

"I don't want your Sunday best," I barked.

"Fine," said the bearded scarecrow and collected his coat. He turned his back on me as he sank into the peeling paint of the dilapidated building. I suspected the structure was sure to soon collapse on the heads of its occupants, old-age pensioners most of them.

"What's your name?" I muttered to myself. "You must have bats in your belfry, man."

—m—

Eustaius.eust@abv.bg   Apr 4 at 10:32 AM
To: AnnaVaughn@gmail.com

Re: financial resources/our daughter's education

Today I talked to Mrs. Lacheva, a math teacher and our daughter's class teacher. She informed me that Anna had got a perfect score on the SAT, a 1600. She can study anywhere she pleases. Please provide financial support.

Eustatius

AnnaVaughn@gmail.com   Apr 4 at 10:38 AM
To: Eustatius.eust@abv.bg
Re: financial resources/our daughter's education.

I intended to politely decline your request but decided against it.
I am not interested in talking to you anymore.
Don't text me.
If our daughter needs financial support, she'd better ask for it in an appropriate manner; otherwise, she will receive nothing from me.
You can give her some constructive advice.

Anna

Eustaius.eust@abv.bg   Apr 4 at 10:42 AM
To: AnnaVaughn@gmail.com
Re: our daughter's education.

Give her money.
I miss you.
You are the only woman I have ever missed.

E

AnnaVaughn@gmail.com 4 April, 10:44 AM
To: Eustatius.eust@abv.bg

Re: our daughter's education.

I am not swallowing the bait.
It would be only a matter of time before well-to-do
fools, middle-aged and older, succumbed to your
charms. You are:
Pathetic;
Untalented.
You flatly refused to influence our daughter.
You will not get a penny from me.

Anna

Eustatius.eust@abv.bg   4 April, 10:47 AM
To: AnnaVaughn@gmail.com
Re: our daughter's education.

You are:
Plain
No one but me is Eustatius. Remember that.
Eust.

—∞—

This detail should have been a kick in my dumb head. It sure
had set alarm bells ring, but hurrying forward, I didn't hear anything.
Not a thistle stuck into my back, no hedge branch ripped the baggy
T-shirt I'd put on before I ran towards Road 109. With ease, I got over
the parking lot barrier. No one stopped me. This should be another
kick in the head — I'd noticed that the minute details, rather than the
difficult targets, took the bread out of your mouth. Details opened the
castle gate for you or destroyed your empire. Details, like curiosity,
killed the cat. You are that cat. Details are the true face of death.

A ladder was propped against the lamppost. Someone had carefully pruned the lovely Chinese or Vietnamese sour cherry trees, or maybe Mali cherry trees — how the devil should I know which, although devils had long been the most innocent creatures in the world. I didn't have to climb the lamppost — another "Are you crazy, Anna?" question. A sign. I failed to notice it, and approached the "forgotten" ladder. Well, would you forget a helipad and a man-made lake in a backyard? I scrambled up to the top of the ladder in three seconds, sat on the lamp — what distance was that damn light fixture from the terrace? That day, a safety net, a tangle of strong polythene ropes, dangled to the ground from the obnoxious pots and plants. I could easily catch hold of the net and throw myself on the terrace.

I immediately did so.

For ten seconds, I hung like a rag above the walkway, then pushed myself up, kicking my heels off the wall. It was easy. There was a chair on the terrace, thank you, Lord! Lightning-fast, I secured the thing on the table I knew well, slipped through the window and landed like an elephant in the servants', i.e. service staff's, lavatory. Another warning sign I ignored: this time I forced my way into the house three times faster, and my legs and arms didn't hurt like before.

Quietly, like cheese ripening in my fridge I exchanged for a B+ essay, I padded down to Nikolai's room. Leaning over the poet's lovely face, Rosen knelt on the floor next to Nikolai's pillow, barking quietly, his beard red and scary like a forgotten electric heater that had set the carpet on fire. I stared dumbstruck. A melody, great and bright, rippled and mixed with the snarls in the big man's throat. Then it died. Rosen massaged Nikolai's neck as he crooned his dreamlike piece. The giant's hair had grown long, orange, almost the color of red rust, thick and wiry. A formidable sight. Nikolai hadn't shaved. His pale face was hidden beneath a layer of thin dark hairs. His eyes looked huge and so magnificent I could have cried. Rosen growled.

Unexpectedly, the wailing stopped, Rosen tucked Nikolai in bed, adjusted the pillow under his head, kissed his forehead, and softly, as if he had a baby or a snake in front of him, started to sing. The song was unbelievable. It felt like you said "goodbye" to a good man you'd never see again. You knew that man was dying. No. It was something different. A little boy had no mother and no home in Rosen's voice. I had never heard anything like it. I could not breathe, it was so beautiful.

The song ended as quickly as it had burst forth. Rosen scuttled away on all fours. His shorts revealed first the letter **A**, then double **N,** and finally the **A** of my name, which looked big and powerful on his belly. Maybe Rosen was hungry. My name understood that, and had trembled with embarrassment.

On all fours, his hands and knees as powerful as tree trunks, Rosen retreated to the door, his hair erupting from his skull as it swept the floor. His nose and mouth turned towards Nikolai. He lay submissively, his eyes sad as death, the way one of the poet's female fans had pointed out. Before Rosen slipped out of the room, he kissed the floor the color of the sun. On one of the big man's ankles, I read: **R-O-S-E-N**. On his other ankle, next to the tattoo of a naked boy, I read another name **N-I-K-O-L-A-I.**

Rosen slowly stood up, barked meekly and forlornly as he dressed — a pure white T-shirt, a pure white sweatshirt, pure white socks, and put on his pure white sneakers. Just as sparklingly clean, Nikolai had paid a visit to our school to read us a sonnet from his poetry collection. His poetry scared me. Lots of words that gave you a headache.

When the footsteps of the white sneakers and the rustle of the white T-shirt faded, the stairwell was full of barks and howls. I say "barks" because I couldn't describe these sounds as a song. I could have called them an autumn day or the fear that returned to Nikolai's green eyes. I stood up. Cautiously, I approached the center of Nikolai's galaxy, the youth sculptured out of sun-wood.

Nikolai watched my new jacket fall to the floor, a brown velvet thing that the tight-fisted shopkeeper gave me. Her son had earned an A with my essay on Shelley's *Ode to the West Wind*. I bet the shopkeeper's heir didn't know who Shelley was, or what the word "ode" meant. In addition to the velvet jacket, the woman gave me a bag full of tights, a pair of jeans, and shoes, as good as new, with only a couple of scuffs and scratches. Episodes like that happened to me pretty often. Yesterday, I went to the crummy neighborhood milk shop, and they shoved a packet of cheese in my pocket. The daughter got a B on her math test. I had let her copy the problems I had solved. Other happy parents left me a sack of garlic I later sold at the Frog Market, still others gave me bicycle tires, even men's underpants out of gratitude that their offspring were doing so well in English literature after they'd bought the essays I'd done for them.

Nikolai watched as my new red jersey flared up and, in less than a second, became a pool of blood on the carpet. Apparently, the poet's mind ran away from me. His gaze was dead to my presence. I towered over him. His eyes were on fire, but the flames were not for me. I studied his white skin and I stroked his beard. It was black. My fingertips explored his ribs and the mystic line of his collarbone. I'd never have enough of looking at him. He lay still in his superb whiteness, protected by his god, and did not care for me.

I liked the bowl of weakness he melted in. I was scared he might die as I caressed his limp arms. He was chained to poetry, but poetry made no difference to me. How does a ginkgo seed become a plant? It needs a hundredth of a water drop to strike root. You can bury the seed in the sand, put it under a stone, or use radiation to kill it. It survives. It remains strong. The little seed finds life for itself in its own death. It rises from the dead. It lives on. I found a place for myself. I looked for it in the cold nights and in the days of hunger. In the sheer lack of interest in me I'd spotted something to be strong with. I clung to it, the thing I liked. His green eyes.

It was about time I stood up. But before I did, I looked for a minute longer at the eyes, the beard, the shoulders, for which my thank you didn't mean anything. I waited for the poet to say, "Go away," so I could throw him into the thirsty, dried blood of my T-shirt on the floor of incredible wood. He said nothing, so I shouldn't leave, I thought to myself. I stopped looking at the face that was as beautiful as a young river. I knew that if I stayed on, I would never learn to fly, but I didn't look at the door. I pressed my face against his shoulders, touched his ribs, and bit his fine skin I envied him so much. He had to be the beggar, not me. He had to be hungry. That was impossible, I saw. He who was thirsty wanted water. He didn't. He wouldn't leave the room with the statue of the naked youth nailed to the floor. Nikolai. The ginkgo biloba seed would survive on moisture less than one-hundredth of a raindrop. It would live on. It would sprout new leaves.

I averted my gaze from Nikolai's face. If I had continued to stare at him, self-pity would have turned my thoughts into an empty nest.

I was hungry. I was lonely. Nikolai was not a lake I could swim in. He was not even a swamp. He was frozen, and magnificent under my fingers.

"That's enough!" an icy female voice said.

"What?"

"Stop it!" the voice ordered.

I turned around. Standing before me, tall and slender, was the prettiest woman I had ever seen. Green eyes, green robe, black hair, smooth skin similar to the poet's, whose silhouette, to me, was the image of pure beauty. Nikolai's skin! If you looked at him for a minute, you'd know what you wanted to do. If you looked on, you wouldn't be sure, but you'd do it all the same, and if your skin was thin, you'd probably drop dead.

My heart was strong.

My mind was hunger. My impatience was a wound, and there was no medicine for it. The blood in my veins was more courageous than the woman's green robe, and obstinate like her green words.

"Get out of his bed, or I'll order the bodyguard to kick you out. He'll tie you up."

The woman looked so much like Nikolai that I imagined he had given birth to her; he had carried her under his cool skin more than nine months, probably nine years.

She was a quarrelsome Cleopatra, pretty and unbearable.

Nikolai had sunk into silence, and I knew his thoughts were miles away from my velvet coat — Tana, a classmate's mother, had given it to me in exchange for my grade B essay I did for her daughter. I detached myself from the cold knees of Cleopatra's son. Anemic verse failed to fascinate me.

"I have a proposition for you," the Madonna announced, her voice suddenly a mellifluous church bell at Easter.

Easter was my favorite holiday. Grandma Nada and I dyed nine Easter eggs and kept the most beautiful one for St. Mary, who had always appeared quiet and friendly to me. I liked the icon she was smiling at me from, and for a long time I spoke to no one. I watched her hug the baby in her arms, and loved her for that. Grandmother Nada and I went to St. Nicholas church and lit a 20-cent candle each. Grandma prayed for good health, I prayed too, filled with gratitude that the Mother of God loved her son so much. Her dark eyes comforted me. Grandma Nada and I ate all the eggs, and the Easter cake. At lunch, we drank the bottle of Coca-Cola the manager of the CA supermarket had given me — her daughter had gotten an A on my essay on integrity.

Grandma and I baked meatballs, worth 96 cents each, at the CA supermarket. The saleswoman sold them to me for twenty cents apiece — just to encourage me to start thinking about — she couldn't remember what exactly I should be thinking about.

"You've been the brainy one," she said. "They say you're wacky. It's OK with me. They work your ass off, but they pay you well. I'll pay you well too. Do an essay for a B in English and write my son's math homework for five days. I'll be giving you a box of chocolates at a very good price for a month. What do you say?"

Grandma Nada and I ate the chocolates in her one-room flat and drank Coke to her granddaughters' health in Spain and her grandson's in Germany. We drank water to Grandma Nada's beautiful mind and milk to my beautiful hair. Then we drank more water and ate all our baked rice. It was the most wonderful holiday. That was why I sometimes loved Our Lord — for the holidays He gave us. Then I could stay with Grandma Nada all day long.

Someone was walking to the door. Who could that be? The bodyguard, of course. I heard it all clearly: Rosen's footsteps, his yips and barks, a slight noise like cockroaches crawling on the hardwood floor, but here hardly any bad insects lived.

"I called Rosen, the bodyguard, as I told you I would."

"I'm not afraid of bodyguards."

"Stay away from my son!" Cleopatra said.

I am very fond of being ordered about. Occasionally, my mother and father have tried this approach on me. Taking orders is the love of my life. I left Nikolai to revel in the perfection of his mom's backside. More than anything else, I needed an insolent tone of voice. I was used to twenty-four pairs of eyes ogling me. My dearest classmates! All attempts to intimidate me had failed, though. Nikolai maintained a stony silence.

"Well?" Cleopatra breathed at one point.

"'I need a pen. Rosen!'" I said, and the giant's dragging footsteps halted at the door. "Rosen, bring me something to write a few sentences with, please."

Rosen barked softly, a little puppy that had lost the way and didn't know where his kennel was. The poor thing couldn't understand why he'd never smell his mother's milk again.

"Hey! Take the pen," Rosen growled at me.

I took it and slowly, carefully, so as not to damage Nikolai's flawless skin, wrote THANK YOU under the poet's collarbone.

Then I sat down on the chair of sun-colored wood, probably more expensive than my bachelor flat.

"I know you passed SAT 1 and SAT 2 practice tests with flying colors," the woman said, her voice a bucket of ice. "'I also know you have no money. In the evenings, you collect discarded crates at the Frog Market and sell them for 10 cents apiece in front of the bank. You do essays for numbskulls and earn a pittance."

In case a lady (lady my foot!) knows something, I leave her knowledge well alone. You wouldn't want to teach an old dog new tricks.

"You cannot pay for your education. You're good for nothing, a greasy grind."

"I am what I am," I said. "Apart from that, I am sure you are unable to do essays for numbskulls."

Why didn't I smell a rat an hour ago? All thistles had been permanently killed, letting me squeeze through the hedge with my eyes shut; a ladder waiting for me propped against the lamppost; a convenient net dangling from the terrace under the hideous flower pots; a comfortable chair jutting out by the railing from which I could jump into the servants' bathroom. These details were a rope tied around my neck. A woman with a magical gaze was staring at me, a goddess one felt like making love to, or tearing into pieces if one's name was Anna like mine.

"If my son got you pregnant…" the woman began, her green eyes sinking lovingly into Nikolai's. "If you give birth to his child and sell the baby to me, that is to say, provide me with the little one and sign the necessary documents…"

At this point, Rosen barked as if someone had hit him hard with the livery Nikolai had bought him. A livery is a special uniform worn by a servant. The garment was very French and very chic. Admittedly, it gave a sartorial elegance to the bodyguard. I knew where the name ANNA was tattooed — under exactly which part of the outfit.

"If I adopt the child, I will pay what is necessary for your education in the United Kingdom."

Rosen barked again, and I was grateful to him for that.

It was high time I stood up.

"However, your expenses in the UK will be covered if you have been taught to be frugal," the woman added. "You could study as much as you want. You can go on one condition: the baby must be healthy and normal."

Rosen howled. With astonishing refinement — taking into account the size of his abdominal and thigh muscles — he crossed the room and lowered his head to Nikolai's lips. I thought the giant was going to kiss him, but he didn't. Without asking permission, he massaged the poet's torso, stomach, and arms, the giant fingers dancing beautifully like butterflies.

"This is the first payment in the installment plan I have approved, a tenth of the whole amount," Cleopatra's irresistible eyes gleamed as she spoke. I thought of Tchaikovsky's *Swan Lake*. Her hand sank into the pocket of her dressing gown which was as green as the moment of conception; however, instead of thoughts of conception, I was presented with a bundle of money.

"Is this enough?" she asked.

I kept mum. The white swan offered another moment of conception consistent with her general behavior — a large wad of bills.

"The baby will be checked for birth defects. If he or she is abnormal or exhibits symptoms of psychomotor retardation," the aging belle continued, "you will only keep the amount of money you'd spent during pregnancy on food, vitamins, and consultations with a gynecologist of proven professional standing. You will buy articles I approve of, and of course, I will need receipts. If the child dies, you will cover the cost of its funeral."

It was dark behind the windowpane, but Rosen hardly gave fig about it. He was massaging Nikolai's legs, crooning, and barking, his face a puddle of happy smiles.

I envied the giant his contact with the translucent skin of the thighs.

Soon it would be midnight, the most appropriate time to conceive a child.

—◊◊◊—

Too bad I met again that guy from the Chasm, our swamp.

"What's your name?" he asked me.

"You don't need to know."

"You are Anna," he said. "I asked after you. I'm Dimo. Pleased to meet you." His hair was shorter, and he had shaved. "I've come back from Madrid."

"Why should I want to know?" I had put on a pair of ugly grey trousers, the kind the cleaners from City Utilities and Hygiene Company wore as they swept the floors of the City Hall and washed the toilets. I'd struggled into a thick woolen sweater. It was a straight jacket, that damned article of clothing was, more of sandpaper than wool. I did smell good, I was sure of it. I'd written an essay on Goethe for a B, but the composition turned out to be better than I expected, and the girl I did it for got an A. She paid me handsomely, and crazy as a loon that I was, I for once bought a bottle of perfume, and not from Second

Chance. It was the first time I had been so stupid. Persistently, a scent wafted from me so magnificently that Dimo coughed.

"That stink scares me," he said. "It doesn't smell like you."

Dusk fell and built a home for the sunset. The sun, a yellow safety pin, tried to pierce the clouds and run away, but failed. I'd written so many essays for different people that the noun "sun" lulled me to sleep. The two trees in front of my building were planted half a century ago, far apart, but embers must have been smoldering between their roots from the time they were seeds. Today their shadows rushed toward each other and touched before the night took the city. That was right, sunsets were the happy moment for the trees.

My bachelor flat, Grandma, God bless her soul, left it to me a week before she closed the earth behind her.

"Come," Dimo, said. "I don't want you to smell like that. Please take me to your place. Cook soup for me, please."

"There's no hot water," I said.

There was nothing in my narrow, one-room flat. How could I take anybody there? If you turned around you'd crash your head against a wall. If I warmed the place a little with the electric heater, I called Granma Nada and she came. We talked and cooked and were warm together. I was used to washing and bathing with cold water.

I took Domo to my bachelor flat.

"I hate that smell," he said.

He pulled at my thick sandpaper sweater, helped me out of it, and threw the thing on the floor. "I don't want you to wear those pants either."

I was freezing, and that was only natural. The cockroaches in the building had kicked the bucket in the cold winter.

We ran to the shower. The water was ice and cut me like a knife. I wanted to get rid of the scent and showered longer than my usual ten seconds. It didn't work.

Dimo had to go back to Spain, and work there for three months.

"It's crazy to leave you with that bottle of stink" he said. "What will become of you if you wear perfume in your skin and not me?"

I couldn't cook. He had a sweater, thick as a wall, but soft. "I'll give it to you," he said, but it was a gargantuan thing, way too big for me.

I put on his shirt, black as happy dog's eyes, then slipped into a pair of his pants he'd left in my chest of drawers. They didn't cling to me, those pants, and he tied them up around my waist with his belt.

"You look like a scarecrow," he told me. "Now you can cook me something."

I did. I fried eggs, but not in butter because I had none. I used sunflower oil instead. A pity I forgot them on the stove. Dimo didn't get up to check what was happening. He lay on the mattress on the floor and looked at me — I, hardly able to walk in the huge sweater and his giant pants. A real scarecrow. But Dimo wasn't scared. He ate the eggs and guzzled the bread I'd left on the table. The tablecloth was as old as the Gladiator Revolt of Spartacus in that wonderful movie. As Dimo swallowed the last bite of bread, he muttered, "I want to bathe you again."

"No hot water," I said.

"I'll bathe you with my eyes," he whispered.

He didn't want to leave for Madrid, the city as hot as boiling milk.

"I need money," Domo said. "I'll buy you clothes. Not from Second Chance, and not from Stannoy at the Frog Market. I want to buy you the most expensive dress. The best one. You're my girl. I'll be waiting for you at the place where you were the saddest thing."

Then Dimo left.

He didn't call once, didn't text me, and his phone number was always outside the network coverage.

I wrote essays for a fiver, accepted used prom dresses and sold them to Stannoy, the meanest man at the Frog Market. Grandma Nada and I cooked nettle soup, or baked chicken and rice. Her legs hurt and I helped her carry her meager merchandise to the market. She had no stall. She sat on a plastic crate I had given her, and waited all day for some would-be customer to buy a bundle of sorrel leaves or nettles I'd picked on the steep bank of the Struma River. Now I was nobody's girl, but if you write essays, you fear no one.

Sunset is the wait for a new sunrise, I consoled myself. And the sunrise is the only son of the day. Soon I was going to graduate from school. Then who would I write essays for?

"Don't worry. Someone will always want you to write something," Grandma Nada reassured me. "If no one wants your things, you'll write for me. Look how much money I made today. I sold four bunches of sorrel!" and she showed me her black purse, battered and old like that great movie about the Gladiator Revolt of Spartacus. "We have money for two days! Don't be afraid. Look here, young nettle will soon sprout leaves!"

More young nettles sprouted leaves.

We often made fairytales, Grandma Nada and I. This was our favorite one.

—❧—

THE OLD WOMAN WOULD suddenly turn to me, "Look, I found this outside the building." Then she'd give me a crumpled package. Some words were always scratched on it. "You look at it, Annie," the dear old thing would add. "I lost my glasses again."

I wanted to tell her we had to stop this.

"Oh, Stannoy will have new glasses for you," I said instead.

On the package Grandma Nada gave me, a few words were scribbled, in the ugliest handwriting you could imagine, "A sweater for my girl".

We really had to stop it.

Dimo never called.

—⁂—

A MAN WAS WALKING along Road 109. His jacket was heavy, although the day was warm, and didn't feel like November. The man had polished his shoes, a thing people in this part of town rarely did.

He was a construction worker, an obscure one. He'd written a thousand poems in his mind. Only two of them had been published.

The shabby apartment houses were gone. The man looked at the piles of broken bricks, his heart skipping a beat. Anna's house was gone, and Road 109 was no more.

"An apartment house used to stand here," the stranger said to a man who wore clean pants that smelled like a second-hand store. "There was an apartment house here, five floors," the stranger added.

"They knocked it down," the local guy said. "Someone bought the land. They don't want us here."

The stranger who obviously hadn't been around for a long time, muttered, "A woman lived in that house. Anna was that woman's name."

"The one who bought the land and knocked our houses down is called Anna," the man blurted out.

"She was poor. A thin, black-haired woman," the stranger said.

"She went to college in the UK. A thin, black-haired bitch," the local guy said.

"Anna…" breathed the stranger.

He must have a screw loose, the guy in the second-hand clothes thought, but he didn't feel sorry for the newcomer. So many folks in this town had lost their marbles. Pity a madman and you'll become a nutcase yourself.

———

ANNA! I'VE BEEN THINKING about it for a long time.

There is one point in common between the beggar and the millionaire, between the ignorant guy and the genius. It's the billions of years that have turned bacteria into human beings. The evolution of a hundred billion years is the common ground between the aristocrats who live in palaces, and the homeless folks who sleep under bridges. There is an amoeba in each one of us — in the coalminer and in the merchant, in the surgeon and in his patient — but there is also the heart of a human being.

I wrote a poem for you. It's called *To Weave a Grasshopper's Cage*.

You told me the grasshopper dies if you put him in a cage.

Anna!

With the amoeba that's hiding in me and with everything human in my blood, I am looking for you. Where are you?

149

Where are you!

I have been told that if you think of someone, of a woman, you sooner or later find her.

During the billions of years that I have been whatever the wind has wanted me to be, I have looked for you — whatever you have been. We'd flown together in the clouds, we'd swum in the ocean and among the stars — if there were stars — ever since I started looking for you.

"Mom, I already have a girl," I told my mother. "You may not like her, but she's my girl."

Anna. In November, when it's really autumn, I go to the lake every night.

You used to swim in that lake.

I'm waiting for you on the shore. They say they're going to pump out the water to clear the way. As long as there is a lake there, I will come. When there is no lake, I will come again. I'll be coming for you for a billion years. Trust me. I'll be looking for you until I become dust.

I'll be dust, and I will become a man again, and I will find you.

I love you.

About the Author

Zdravka Evtimova is a Bulgarian writer born in 1959. Her short stories and novels have appeared in 31 countries in the world, including USA, UK, Canada, China, Australia, Germany, France, Japan, Italy, and Switzerland. In 2022, she won Romania's Mihai Eminescu Annual Award for Fiction.

Fomite

More novels and novellas from Fomite...

Joshua Amses
 During This, Our Nadir
 Ghats
 Raven or Crow
 The Moment Before an Injury
Raymond Barfield
 Dreams of a Spirit Seer
Charles Bell
 The Married Land
 The Half Gods
Jaysinh Birjepatel
 Nothing Beside Remains
 The Good Muslim of Jackson Heights
David Borofka
 The End of Good Intnetions
David Brizer
 Cacademonomania
 The Secret Doctrine of V. H. Rand
 Victor Rand
L. M Brown
 Hinterland
Paula Closson Buck
 Summer on the Cold War Planet
Ann Abelson/L.enny Cavallaro
 Paganini Agitato
Dan Chodorkoff
 Loisaida
 Sugaring Down
David Adams Cleveland
 Time's Betrayal
Paul Cody
 Sphyxia
Jaimee Wriston Colbert
 Vanishing Acts
Roger Coleman
 Skywreck Afternoons
Stephen Downes
 The Hands of Pianists
Marc Estrin
 Et Resurrexit

Fomite

Fomite

Fomite

Writing a review on social media sites for readers will help the progress of independent publishing. To submit a review, go to the book page on any of the sites and follow the links for reviews. Books from independent presses rely on reader-to-reader communications